Further Praise for *Unformed Landscape*

"Swiss novelist Stamm's spare, uncluttered, deceptively simple prose evokes a cinema verité quality: we are drawn into Kathrine's world and can almost feel her struggles to grow up."

—*Library Journal*

"One of the most eerily beautiful road stories to emerge in European fiction in years."

—*Philadelphia Weekly*

"This brief Swiss-authored novel . . . is one of quiet power and understated tension."

—*Playback STL*

"This is a novel of great delicacy, by turns chilling and tender, and full of subtle surprises."

—James Lasdun, author of *The Horned Man*

"Set in a world with which few readers will be familiar— the winter-darkened landscape north of the Arctic Circle—Peter Stamm's *Unformed Landscape* tells the deceptively simple story of a young woman's first, brief journey into what is for her 'the south.' But this beautiful novel is more than that: an eloquent exploration of how disillusionment can give rise to bravery, and a testament to the virtues of understatement."

—David Leavitt, author of
The Body of Jonah Boyd: A Novel

UNFORMED
LANDSCAPE

Peter Stamm

Translated by
Michael Hofmann

HANDSEL BOOKS

an imprint of
Other Press • New York

We wish to express our appreciation to Pro Helvetia, Arts Council of Switzerland, for their assistance in the preparation of the translation.

PRO●HELVETIΛ
■Γ
Arts Council of Switzerland

Production Editor: Robert D. Hack
Text design: Kaoru Tamura
This book was set in Sabon by Alpha Graphics of Pittsfield, NH.
First softcover printing 2006
ISBN-13: 978-1-59051-226-5
ISBN-10: 1-59051-226-X

10 9 8 7 6 5 4 3 2 1

Library of Congress Cataloging-in-Publication Data

Stamm, Peter, 1963–
[Ungefähre Landschaft. English]
Unformed landscape / by Peter Stamm ; translated by Michael Hofmann.
    p. cm.

ISBN 1-59051-140-9 (hardcover : alk. paper)
I. Hofmann, Michael, 1957 Aug. 25-   II. Title.
PT2681.T3234U6413 2005
833'.914–dc22

                                    2004013577

UNFORMED

LANDSCAPE

T he nights were no longer properly dark, it was April. Kathrine had gotten up early, even though it was Saturday. She woke her son, fixed him his breakfast, and took him to his grandmother. She went home, buckled on her cross-country skis, and set off. She followed the snowmobile tracks until she reached the first height, and after that the wires that led up to the radio mast. Finally, after perhaps an hour, she moved away from that last landmark at a sharp angle, and glided out into the limit-less white of the fjeld.

At around noon she sat down to rest and have something to eat on a rock that broke through the snow. She ran her hands over the orange, yellow, and white lichens that covered the stone.

Later on, when she was on the trail again, there was a sort of misty haze, and the sky lost its blueness, and got paler and paler. But she knew the way, she had been to the lighthouse many times, and even when the sun was finally gone from sight, and the light was so diffuse that everything blurred, she went on, and wasn't afraid of losing her way.

Kathrine had married Helge, she had had a child, she had divorced Helge. She went to the lighthouse, she stayed there overnight, and came back the next day. Her mother would look after the boy then, as she did during the days when Kathrine was at the customs office.

After work, she went to her mother's. The three of them would eat supper together, later Kathrine would pick up the child and go home. Eventually, the child learned to walk, and she didn't have to carry him anymore. That was in summer. Then the days grew shorter, autumn came, the first snow, and then winter.

The sun had disappeared weeks ago, and it no longer got light at all. Night lay over the landscape. The village was locked in darkness. The light of the streetlamps was like a space that no one left. It was forty kilometers to the nearest village, eighty on the road that led through the dead landscape into the interior and back to the coast.

When it snowed, when it did nothing but snow, the road was closed. And then the little airport outside the village on a small plateau was also closed, and there were no buses and no flights, only the Hurtig Line vessels heading south in the evenings, and late at night to Kirkenes on the Russian border.

It often snowed, and it was cold and dark. Kathrine's father died, one morning he didn't wake up. He wasn't even very old. The pastor came and sat in the kitchen with her mother. Kathrine made coffee, then she took the child by the hand and went home. The pastor and her mother were still sitting in silence at the kitchen table.

On Sunday the pastor spoke of the water of life that poured out into the sea of eternity. Then, he said, every creature living there will swim freely. There will be quantities of fish. Because as soon as this water comes, the salt water will heal, and everything the river touches will remain alive forever.

Then the congregation went outside, and went through the darkness and the deep snow to the cemetery. They had had to heat the soil for four days before the gravediggers had been able to shovel the grave.

Spring came late that year. Kathrine had her twenty-fifth birthday in the autumn. Her mother baked her a cake as she did every year, and on Saturday they all went to the Elvekrog and had a party that was the talk of the village for long afterward.

On Monday Kathrine inspected the *Verchneuralsk*. She had been in the office only a little while, writing a report, when the boss sent her out. The weather was stormy that day, out at sea the waves were high as houses, and everything that could sought the shelter of port. Thirty trawlers had already anchored, including some that had only meant to come back a week later. The boss had thrown away the faxes from the Coast Guard and said today's going to be a hard day for everyone, today you're all going to have to go out.

The ships lay in the harbor, or were moored to the floating dock the Russians had built at the edge of the village. Groups of Russian sailors were standing all over the village. They stood there waiting and talking, and the villagers crossed to the other side of the street. The Russians were standing outside Rimi, and outside the other supermarket. They stood in front of the kiosk, they looked in the windows of the computer shop and the ship's electronic shop. When Kathrine drove to the port, she stopped to search a group of Russians. Sometimes they would carry vodka in their plastic bags, or contraband cigarettes, that they would sell in the village.

The *Verchneuralsk* had already been unloaded. Kathrine knew she wouldn't find anything on board, not vodka, not cigarettes, but she always boarded the ship each time it was in port, regardless. Then Alexander, the captain, would ask her into his tiny cabin, and take down the table from its two hooks on the ceiling. He sat on the bunk, and left the chair to Kathrine, and they would talk a little, even though they could hardly understand each other. Each time, Alexander would offer her vodka, and each time she declined. She tried to explain to him that she wasn't permitted to accept any hospitality from him, but he just laughed, and poured for her anyway, and she left it untouched. Then Alexander would make instant coffee and tell her about his wife and his two daughters, Nina and Xenia, about Murmansk, and then he said Kathrine ought to visit him there sometime. It was a beautiful city, he said, and he showed her some post-cards. The Atlantica cinema, the swimming baths, the enor-mous statue of the soldier to commemorate the defenders of the Soviet polar regions in the great patriotic war. Some-times he would take out his photo album, and show her photos of the harbors he had visited, pictures of the Shet-lands, the Faroes, the Lofoten Islands, and he asked Kathrine why she didn't get away from here at last.

"You're young," he said, as if that was a reason to leave, "and you're beautiful."

But she just laughed.

The bad weather moved east. In the middle of the day the thermometer now climbed above zero, and the snow was old and hard. Kathrine went out to the lighthouse, she hadn't been there for a long time. She didn't know who was on duty that month, but it hardly mattered, all the lighthouse keepers were the same anyway. They had been fishermen before, they were unmarried or widowed men who did the job for twenty years and seemed never to get any older, and who then died one day, and it was nothing. They kept the place clean and looked after the equipment and stared out to sea with big binoculars, and watched the ships go by. They were pleased when Kathrine came out to see them. They would talk a lot, tell stories of bygone times, about people who had died or emigrated a long time ago. They always told the same stories, talked uninterruptedly, and still they were as silent as the landscape.

Kathrine went back to the village across the day-wide empty snowscape, past fjords and mountains, over smooth plains and gentle slopes. The fjeld looked like a drawing made of a few scribbled lines. Russia, Finland, Sweden, and Norway, up here they all looked alike. The borders were covered by snow, the snow joined everything up, and the darkness covered it over. The real borders were between day and night, between summer and winter, between the people.

Once, Kathrine saw a few reindeer. They were standing in a little huddle, all looking in the same direction. It was spring, the nights were short and bright, but the snow wouldn't go away until early summer, and then only for a few months.

Kathrine had left Helge because he was a drinker and a violent man. He hadn't ever dared to hit her, but she despised him, and eventually threw him out of their apartment, and he didn't come back. She saw him every day when he came off work in the fish factory, and rode through the village on his old Harley, up to the tenement he now lived in with a couple of other workers, and then down to the port, and up and back down again. Then he would go to the Elvekrog and get drunk, and after midnight Kathrine would hear the sound of the bike for a last time, loud, and then getting quieter, until finally she couldn't hear it anymore.

Sometimes Kathrine would visit a girl friend, or girl friends would visit her, and their children would play together until they were tired, and their mothers carried them home.

The older one became, the harder it was to bear the darkness and the cold. That's what everyone said, and it might well be true. The old people didn't say anything, they sat silently at home, watched television, and waited.

People went visiting, or they received visits. Front doors were left unlocked, and there were always lights on in the windows. They went out in their cars, and drove from house to house. They met in the fishermen's home, or the pub, the Elvekrog. They drank tea and coffee, and told each other stories. They drank beer until they had forgotten the dark.

The men, as the joke had it, didn't want to marry in winter, because then the wedding night would go on for three months. A joke that went around a lot. Why didn't he get married in winter? Because then the wedding night would have lasted for three months.

They married in summer, and in winter they got divorced, and then you spent a night with another man, who would make an effort. A night in another bed, other hands, other words that still came to the same thing. Stay awhile, won't you, come under my blanket, it's cold, turn around. What is it you want? I don't know. Don't say anything.

Kathrine ate lunch with her customs colleagues at the fishermen's home, where Svanhild cooked, and where the agents from the Russian fishing companies sometimes stayed, and the engineers and the seamen when the ships had to be refitted.

At a party in the Elvekrog, Kathrine met Christian, a Dane who was spending a couple of months in the village, to supervise the installation of a new automatic weighing machine in the fish factory. Christian looked exactly the way Kathrine imagined a Dane would look. Everything about him was bright, his eyes, his skin, his hair. He wasn't fat, but his face and hands were soft and indeterminate. He had a mild voice, and a laptop with an Internet connection. Kathrine visited him a couple of times in his apartment on the edge of the village. He showed her his company's home page, and Kathrine waited for him to kiss her, but he didn't kiss her.

Christian left. By now, Kathrine herself had an Internet connection, and they exchanged e-mails for a while. Sometimes Christian's e-mails came from other countries he was visiting to supervise the installation of other pieces of equipment in other fish factories. At first, he would always write enthusiastically about those countries, then he would only write about his work, and eventually his e-mails started coming from Aarhus again, where he lived and where the company he worked for was based.

Kathrine told Alexander about Christian. Alexander had never been to Aarhus, but he had heard it was a beautiful city.

"Why don't you go and see him there sometime?" he asked.

Kathrine laughed.

Alexander said, "You expect too much from other people. You're responsible for your own life."

"Did you study psychology?" asked Kathrine. "You sound like someone who's studied psychology."

"*No problem*," said Alexander, and he drank the vodka he'd poured for Kathrine, and hung the table up from its two hooks on the ceiling.

That evening the *Verchneuralsk* left, and for the first time in months Kathrine went to the pub. She had left the boy with his grandmother. She went home with a man, and spent the night with him. He was a former boyfriend of hers. Two weeks later, the *Verchneuralsk* came back, with its hold full of fish and ice.

Sometimes, when the weather was very bad, Kathrine would listen to the forecast on the radio. The wind strengths and the places, Jan Mayen, Greenland, Svalbard,

Newfoundland, the Pole. Then she would think about Alexander and his crew. Even though she knew the ship quite well, she couldn't imagine it in the darkness, somewhere far out to sea, with the waves crashing over her decks, and the men hauling in nets in the continual rise and dip of the waves, day and night. She hoped they were all right.

It got to be autumn, and winter. The year came to a close, and the next one began. Then it was spring.

This morning was silvery and clear. A strong wind blew off the Barents Sea, and the waves were topped with foam. Christian was working in Portugal now, and he wrote that the peach trees were already in flower there, and that the Portuguese women were quite different from the Danish women or the Norwegian women. Kathrine wrote that she was going to get married again, and Christian offered his congratulations. She was happy when it rained for the first time in the year, and overnight the blanket of snow was half-melted away.

Kathrine married Thomas, they had known each other for just six months. Thomas didn't fancy a honeymoon, he had already been all over. He talked about Africa. He said Africa was his favorite country. When Kathrine said she had never been south of the Arctic Circle, he laughed and said he didn't believe her. It was true, she said.

In the summer, Kathrine and her colleagues caught a Russian who had smuggled ten thousand Ecstasy pills over the border. They arrested him, it wasn't difficult. He smiled, and kept apologizing for the trouble he had put them to. *"No problem,"* he said, when he was put on the ship to Vadso, where he was tried and sent to prison. When he was released, he disappeared, and was never seen in the village again.

Kathrine discussed his case with Alexander. She said that sooner or later every smuggler got caught, and it was dangerous to get mixed up with drug dealers. Alexander laughed and winked at her. She shrugged her shoulders, and ignored the vodka he'd poured for her, and drank the coffee. Alexander said he hadn't been paid in three months. She offered him money, but he refused, and gave her a loaf of Russian bread.

Once, when it was winter again, and a violent storm was blowing at sea, the *Verchneuralsk* stayed in port overnight. Kathrine had visited Alexander in the course of the afternoon. He had given her half a codfish in a plastic bag with ice. That evening, on the way home, Kathrine saw Alexander and his men heading for the pub. She raised the bag with the fish in it, and waved. The men didn't see her. She shouted something to them, but the words were blown away in the gale.

The snow fizzed horizontally through the light shed by the streetlamps. When Kathrine got home, Thomas was already there. He was sitting with the little boy in the kitchen. They were playing a game.

"Here comes Mama," said Thomas, and he kissed Kathrine.

"I've got some cod for tonight," said Kathrine, but the child made a fuss, and then so did Thomas. He said he was going to get hot dogs from the kiosk, and then he disappeared.

The boy was sitting at the table. Kathrine put her arm around his shoulder.

"Have you done your homework?" she asked. "Do you like Thomas?"

"He's nice," said the boy. "We played a game together."

"Did you win?"

"We're still playing," said the boy.

Kathrine moved one of the wooden figures on the board forward a square, and said, "I'll help you." Then the child said, "God sees everything," and moved the figure back, and held it there until Kathrine went out into the corridor to take off her shoes.

"And what shall I do with the fish?" she asked when Thomas came back.

The next day Alexander was reported missing. A woman everyone knew said she had seen him walking out of the village at half past one at night. She said she hadn't been able to sleep. And he had been just the same as ever, not drunk. They looked for Alexander for several days, but didn't even manage to find any traces of him in the snow, and eventually the *Verchneuralsk* left port without him.

Kathrine sat looking out the window in the fishermen's refuge. She walked through the village. The sun hadn't appeared for a couple of weeks now. The lights were on in the windows of the houses. The streetlamps were on night and day, and even the graves in the cemetery had lights on them. At Christmas, Kathrine thought of Alexander's wife and his two daughters. She wanted to write to them, but she didn't know what to say, and so she let it go. Thomas gave Kathrine an electric wok.

Svanhild didn't ask Kathrine why she wanted a room, she only asked her how long she wanted to stay. Kathrine said, "One night, maybe longer," and Svanhild gave her a key. It was late.

The room was small and much too warm, full of a dry electric heat. It had a smell of dust, even though all its surfaces were sealed, the laminated floors, the PVC wall panels, the cheap melamine furnishings.

Kathrine tipped open the window as far as it would go and switched on the television, which was fixed to the wall on a metal arm. She chose an English-language news channel, and turned the volume down so low that she could hear the speaker, but not make out the words. She lay down on the bed. The cover wasn't old, but it was full of cigarette holes and stains that washing had only driven deeper into the material. She stood up and went over to the window. The room was on the lower ground floor, the window was only just above ground level.

Kathrine looked out onto the street she walked down every morning on the way to work. She thought of the people who had been in this room before her, seamen, fishing agents, engineers. Perhaps Christian had slept here his first few nights, before he had found an apartment. Perhaps he had watched her go by in the morning, smoking a cigarette out of the window, from that strange vantage. Before they had met. On one of those winter mornings when you had to look at the clock to know whether it was day yet, or not. When it didn't get light at all, or just an hour or two at midday. Maybe Christian had observed her. She couldn't remember, was it he who had spoken to her in the Elvekrog, or vice versa. She had the feeling that that woman who walked past this window every morning was not herself, the feeling that she had turned into someone else, a stranger, a chance visitor in an unfamiliar village, in a year that had just turned. She had taken the ship on the Hurtig Line, had got off on a whim, and had taken a room. Tomorrow, she would travel on, and forget the name of this village.

Kathrine was confused, and her confusion frightened her. It was as though she had lost all her orientation, as though she had stepped out of her life like a house, a house she was viewing now from the outside, from below, from a foot above the ground, from the point of view of a dog, or a child, the child she had been when her parents had first come to the village. She rambled through her memories. There was no more before and after. Her whole life seemed to lie ahead of her, like this village. All the people she had known were still there, including her father, who had died four years ago, and Alexander, and Christian, who was somewhere in Portugal, or France, or Spain. Nothing changed, nothing had changed. She could go to school, she thought, and attend her early lessons again, and then go on to the Elvekrog, and dance with Helge. He would get her pregnant. Down in the port, the *Verchneuralsk* was docking, Christian was just coming off work in the fish factory, he left town again, the baby was born, Kathrine was sixteen and smoking her first cigarette, was kissing a boy for the first time. She was sitting with Morten in the old German harbor fortifications, and they were looking across at the village and planning a trip to Paris that they would never make. Kathrine was going to the library, taking books out she could not yet understand, that no longer interested her. She was drinking coffee with Alexander. Her father got ill, her son got ill, Kathrine got ill. Helge came home drunk. The winters were endlessly long. Kathrine was visiting her friends, and their kids played together. Then her second marriage, and the celebrations at Thomas's parents. Her mother spent the whole day helping out in the kitchen. When Kathrine came to get her, she refused. She had borrowed an apron from Thomas's mother, and Kathrine felt ashamed for her. Thomas and the other men were sitting in the den, smoking cigars, and the women were sitting in the living room, drinking tea. Kathrine didn't know what to do with herself.

It wasn't until she thought about Thomas that some order came to her thoughts. His life was going somewhere. He had always known what he wanted, and where he was going. He had grown up in Tromso, done well at school, had gone on to college, and worked at a job. Then his grandmother had died, and his parents moved to the village, to their big house, one of the nicest in the village, with a big garden. Thomas's father had taken early retirement, and spent his days reading the Bible and managing his money. Thomas's mother was active in the community, got herself voted onto the school board and the library committee.

Then Thomas came into the village, and became production manager at the fish factory. Kathrine first met him at the church bazaar, where he was helping his mother at the kindergarten stall. They were selling little crafts things the children and the mothers had made in the course of the year. Kathrine was there with her little boy, and Thomas right away started talking to him, but keeping his eyes all the time on Kathrine. She had found him disagreeable then, and hadn't liked the way he was with the child. As if he were the father. The child had liked him, maybe he missed not having a father. That's what everyone always said. The child needs a father.

Later on, Thomas had gone over and joined them when they were all drinking hot chocolate and eating cake in the community center. He had asked whether the chair next to her was free, and then sat down before she could answer. He had talked about himself, about growing up in Tromso, about his travels. Kathrine hadn't liked him any better, but the boy was beaming as he hadn't for a long time, and was all excited. Thomas gave him something, a little toy. Helge was sitting at a corner table with a couple of colleagues. They had brought beer, and were drinking and talking noisily about the bad fish yields of the last few months, and about bikes, and about women. Once, Helge looked across to Kathrine, and grinned at seeing her sitting together with Thomas. Thomas was his boss, but Helge wasn't interested in Kathrine or the baby anymore, not after Kathrine had told him he didn't have to pay her any more maintenance, and just to leave her alone.

Then Thomas had called Kathrine a couple of times, had asked her out for a coffee, and then for dinner. She had accepted the invitations, she no longer remembered why. Maybe, like the little boy, she was dreaming of a family, a big house, and a life free from worries. Then he had invited her back on Sunday, her and the child, to meet his parents. It had been a ghastly occasion, stiff and full of little embarrassments and humiliations. But when Kathrine had stepped out onto the glassed-in balcony to smoke a cigarette, Thomas had come after her and kissed her, and she had kissed him back, in the dull despair that had come over her in that chill house.

Everything thereafter had been a mistake. Kathrine had been overrun by Thomas's purposefulness, dazzled by the stories about his past and his future. That evening they had slept together for the first time, a rushed job in Kathrine's living room, while the child was in the bedroom, playing with a train set Thomas had given him. Thomas had knelt in front of the sofa. He hadn't even taken off his clothes.

That day, Kathrine had met Thomas's sister Veronica, and Einar, her husband. At the time they were living with Thomas's parents, in the big house. Einar owned the little computer store on the main street. But the business wasn't doing well, and Veronica and Einar decided to go back to Tromso. Then Thomas said the apartment in his parents' house would be empty. If we take it, he said, then we can get the whole house, when my parents are dead. But that was later on, when they were already married, and when Thomas was already living with Kathrine.

Thomas knew what he was after. When he started talking about marriage, it hadn't even crossed Kathrine's mind. His life represented a bold stroke through the unformed landscape of her life. Like the pistes for a snowmobile, marked with poles in the snow, his life cut across hers, with an objective and a destination. It was possible that Thomas himself didn't know why he had chosen this particular path, but he had put down the marker poles, and it was a way that could be gone, and that he was going to go with her.

Kathrine was tired. Thomas was certainly in bed by now. He had always been able to sleep. A clear conscience, he sometimes said, and laughed, and Kathrine hadn't understood why. She had a clear conscience. She had never said she loved him. And she didn't have any secrets from him. If there was something he wanted to know, he could ask her. But he never asked her about her life. She wasn't even sure if he knew that she had been married to Helge. What I don't know, he sometimes said, and laughed.

Thomas. That was his name. Her husband. My husband, she thought. He was thirty, two years older than she was. His family was his family. Everything else was a lie. Thomas, my husband, thought Kathrine. By the time they married, they hadn't slept together for months. On their wedding night, she had induced him to do something that he later referred to as playing. But it wasn't a game. And then they didn't talk about it anymore. Thomas avoided the subject, as he avoided the thing itself. The thing, Kathrine said, and she laughed aloud. And since then, another half a year had passed without them sleeping together—or, as she said, making love.

"What did you marry him for?" asked Morten, when she told him about it.

"Because he loved me," Kathrine replied.

My husband, said Kathrine, by the open window, Thomas, my husband. She smiled. A man going by on the opposite side of the road looked across to her, a drunken seaman. He waved, and she waved back. He said something she couldn't make out. She said something that might have been a greeting or a suggestion. The man shook his head, and went on. Kathrine shut the window.

On the upper story of Nils H. Nilsen's fish factory, a few windows were lit up. Where foreign workers lived. Kathrine tried to imagine the rooms behind the windows, and the people who sat there, watched television or read. Who made love or ate dinner. She imagined someone over there looking across to her, to the window where she was still standing. And when she lay down on the bed again, she imagined someone over there seeing the light on in her room, but not seeing her, and wondering who it was who lived there. Continually wondered about it, every night. When every night there was someone different in the room.

Kathrine used to walk past the fishermen's refuge every day. And now she was inside it, sitting by the window, eating the breakfast that was included in the price. When she stepped out on the street, she paused for a moment. It was as though she was waiting for herself, for the Kathrine who hadn't doubted, hadn't asked, hadn't run away, and whose life had continued as before. She looked up the road, in the direction from which she used to come every morning. Then she saw Svanhild clearing the table inside. She waved, and Svanhild waved back and smiled, and Kathrine set off.

She walked down the street, quickly and without looking back. She thought of the day ahead and the work to be done. Her boss was already in the office. He was smoking. She opened the window, made coffee. Later, she picked up the mail, and brought the whole stack to her boss, without looking through it. He liked to do it all himself. It wasn't much, in any case. Then he called her in. "This one's not for me," he said, and handed her an envelope that had his name on it, and two sheets of single-spaced typing. Kathrine read. She read, and sensed her boss looking at her. But he didn't say anything. He waited.

"Don't you dare show your face in our house again, ever. Leave our brother/brother-in-law/son alone! You have abused our hospitality and our trust, and brought filth into our house. We have seen through you, and refuse to be taken in anymore by a rotten bitch like you. Your lewdness and abomination you must bear by yourself."

The telephone rang, but Kathrine only stared at it, her boss stared at it. Kathrine listened to it ringing and ringing, and finally stopping. One of her colleagues left the customs office on his way to inspect a ship that had just come in. Kathrine was still holding the letter in her hand, the second page of it. The first she had dropped onto the table. She read the last few sentences again.

"Good-bye, then, and for good. Catch yourself some other man, but spare Thomas, and spare us. We will not tolerate your presence in our house, under any circumstances! God will punish you for your misdeeds, you whore! Because God knows the path of righteousness; while the path of godlessness leads to destruction."

Kathrine sat down and stood up again. She took a cigarette from her boss's pack, which lay on the desk. He lit it for her. She had dropped the second page of the letter on the desk as well. Her boss picked it up, and read aloud: "Copies of this letter are going to your mother, Thomas, Morten, and anyone else who wants one." He tore up the letter and dropped it in the wastepaper basket. He smiled.

"Brother, brother-in-law, son," he said. "Crazy the lot of them. You can't take it seriously."

It wasn't a question, it was a command.

"I don't know what it's all about, but I never asked for a copy. I regard the matter as closed. I don't want to hear anything about it."

When Kathrine thought about the office now, she could only think of the fitted carpet, which ran up the walls a little way, and always gave her the feeling of not quite having her feet on the ground. It was as though everything in the office had only provisionally been set down on that carpet, and sometimes it would disappear again, when the workers came to roll it up and cart it down to the street, and put it in the dumpster—when the head office in Oslo finally agreed to the long overdue renovation.

He regarded the matter as closed, her boss had said, but Kathrine knew it wasn't, that the letter would forever be lying there, between the two of them, even if he believed, even if he knew it was all a lie.

At around lunchtime, her mother had called her at the office. This was something she had done only once before, when Kathrine's father had died. Kathrine assured her that it was all a lie, and her mother tried to calm her down. But Kathrine sensed the doubt in her voice, and quickly ended the call.

Kathrine had gone out to lunch with her colleagues, as she did every day. She had looked at the other people in the restaurant, and wondered which of them had also received a copy of the letter. But nobody had betrayed any sign. Kathrine had had the sensation of being the only human, among lots of browsing animals. After lunch, she had stayed in the fishermen's refuge and had holed up in her room all afternoon, and cried a lot.

The following day she hadn't gone into work, nor the day after. She stopped going. She hadn't handed in her notice, she just stopped going, and the only thing that surprised her was that she didn't hear from her boss at all.

Kathrine sat in her room in the fishermen's refuge. She thought about the office, about her boss, her colleagues. She looked out the window, and watched the workers going to the fish factory, the children going to school, the women leaving the houses to go shopping. She lay down, and she got up. Then it was already time for the office workers to be coming out of the factory and the town hall, to drink coffee at Svanhild's. A few seamen were on the streets, three old women with Zimmer frames stopped right in front of Kathrine's window, just stood there, not talking, and finally went on.

Once, she heard some noise from next door, and she wondered what it was like for the Russian fishermen who stayed here while their ships were in port, being serviced or repaired. In these rooms with their easy-to-clean, man-made surfaces. A damp cloth would wipe away all traces of them after they were gone, off at sea on one of the rusty trawlers, to live in a tiny cabin for a week or two of hectic work.

Kathrine knew those cabins. She had inspected them often enough. Some of the seamen had pinups on their walls, and turned the music louder when she came along. She felt their eyes on her when she bent down to look under the bunks, and her overalls grew taut across her behind. Some of the time she didn't mind it, and some of the time she felt scared. Others had pictures of saints or the Virgin Mary on their walls. On the bottom deck, where the sailors slept, the men slept three to a cabin. Kathrine looked in the cupboards, pushed aside empty tins of Nescafé. The vodka was usually kept behind the drawers under the bunks. Two or three bottles, rarely more than that. The seamen stood in the doorways. They wore felt slippers and rough knitted vests, and they smiled apologetically and said, *"No problem*," when Kathrine wrote out the receipt for the fine. She felt sorry for the men with their hand-drawn calendars, on which they crossed off the days, and the weeks, and the months until they could go home again. But they had an apartment somewhere, maybe a wife, and one or two kids. They had chests where they kept their clothes, and walls where they had their pictures. They had what Kathrine no longer had.

After Thomas had moved in with her, he had gradually taken over her life and her apartment. He had been generous, and bought expensive, new things. He hadn't liked her furniture, he had mocked her collection of books until she gave them to the library or simply got rid of them. And every time they tidied up—and Thomas liked nothing better than spring cleaning—she noticed that something disappeared, until there was hardly anything left. A dust trap, he said. You never look at that, what's the point of it. She had supposed that was love. She had thought they were building something together, but it was just Thomas building her into his life, trying to mold her, to train her, until she suited him, and suited the type of life he planned to lead. Until her own apartment was as foreign to her as his parents' house, as he was, and as the life she led with him.

Kathrine had been living in the fishermen's refuge for four days when the letter came. She stayed another three. She didn't go into the office anymore. She sat in her room, and only left it to get something to eat, in the afternoons, when there was hardly anyone left in the restaurant. Svanhild didn't ask any questions, but she was very friendly, sometimes she just stood next to the table while Kathrine was eating, without saying anything. After a week, Kathrine moved back into the apartment.

She noticed right away that Thomas had moved out, that the apartment was empty, even though there was nothing missing. Presumably, he was back with his parents, in the rooms that had been set aside for the three of them, that he had fixed up weeks ago, and never wanted to show her. A surprise. Our nest, he had once said, a snug nest for us.

Kathrine stood in the apartment, on which they had already canceled the lease. In two weeks, at the end of January, she would have to go. The potted plants were all dry, and presumably past saving. The key to the mailbox lay on the kitchen table. When Kathrine opened the fridge, a sour smell wafted out. She emptied the rest of a milk carton into the sink, picked up a half-eaten bar of chocolate, and sat down in the living room. She opened the mail from the past days, some junk mail, a Christmas card from Christian in Boulogne, France. It was pretty there, he wrote, but he was going back to Aarhus in a couple of days. Then Kathrine read the letter from Thomas's family, which they had copied to her here as well. She read it again.

"Hated Kathrine, how long have you been playing your mean games with our brother/brother-in-law/son? Are two lawful husbands not enough for you, must you amuse yourself with other men too, so blinded by lust that they agree to play your games? You go hopping from one bed to another, just exactly the way you feel like, and as fancy takes you. You're a deceitful snake. In bygone ages, people would stone harlots like you, but we, we pray for you, that God in His great mercy may forgive you your unchastity."

Kathrine read the letter from beginning to end, read the signatures, every name, every letter. They had all set their names to it—Thomas's parents, his sister Veronica, and Einar, his brother-in-law. Kathrine was put in mind of death announcements in the newspapers, in which brothers, sisters, children, nieces, and nephews all took their leave of the deceased. She herself was mother, daughter, sister-in-law, and daughter-in-law. A divorced and remarried wife. Then she thought of Einar, the brother-in-law. Einar, of all people. Kathrine laughed, and was surprised at the sound of her laughter in the quiet apartment. It wasn't her laugh at all. She laughed to hear herself laughing. Strange, she thought, that you cry alone, but never laugh. I've never laughed alone before.

She felt certain that it was Einar who had written the letter. She remembered the evening he had kissed her goodbye on the mouth, the feeling of the tip of his tongue between his thin, dry lips, the smell of his breath when he talked to her, and got far too close to her. A smell she couldn't describe, and the very thought of which still disgusted her today.

She imagined Thomas reading the letter, back home with his parents. She thought of how he'd always brought the mail into the kitchen. He had insisted on being the one who always emptied the mailbox, even when Kathrine got home before he did. When he had moved in with her, he had made some joke, and taken the key to the mailbox off her key ring. He got the mail, took the big knife out of the kitchen drawer, and slashed open all the letters, one after another. He took them out of their envelopes, opened them out, and smoothed them down with his hand. He punched holes in them, and only then would he read them, one after another, and afterward he would file them away in his binders.

Kathrine punched holes in the letter from Thomas's family, pulled down the binder labeled "T. family" off the bookshelf, and filed the letter. She smiled as she thought Thomas would be satisfied with her work. But he would certainly have read the letter too, perhaps before it was sent, perhaps he had even helped write it. Only he hadn't signed it.

There was also a file marked "K. family." Thomas had started it for Kathrine, even though she never got mail from her family. Her father had broken with his own family over some old incident sometime, and it was a wonder that they had showed up at his funeral. And her mother's family had never been happy about her marriage, and contact was limited to birthday and Christmas cards, and the occasional telephone call.

When Kathrine saw the file for the first time, she had laughed. Then she noticed it was one of Thomas's little bits of malice, one of the innumerable bits of malice he perpetrated every day, when he took the two files and weighed them in his hands, "K. family" and "T. family."

Kathrine had detested Thomas's family right from the start. The way they behaved to Thomas and Kathrine from the first day. As though they were already married. The off-color remarks during lunch and afterward, and the way they didn't shut the door when they went to the bathroom, and wandered around the house in their underwear when Kathrine was visiting, even the first few visits. Look what a progressive family we are! And the way they talked about money the whole time. See how well off we are! And the feeling they tried to give her that Thomas was quite a catch for her. As a single mother. And with her background.

Kathrine had grown up as an only child. Once, she'd taken Thomas back to her mother. They had spent a nice afternoon together, and gone ice fishing. But after that, Thomas had always found excuses, and her mother hadn't minded that Thomas never came to visit again. Go to him, she said, what would you do here anyway, his parents' house is so much bigger.

They had visited his family continually. There was always something going on—holidays, a birthday, a summer party. They were continually in his parents' big house, and Kathrine had forever had to listen to what a wonderful family it was, and how everyone stuck together, and how stupid and bourgeois all the other people in the village were.

The big house had a sauna, and sometimes when Kathrine was visiting, the father had lit the furnace and said, right, now we're all going to the sauna. At first Thomas hadn't wanted to go, but then his father had said, before the Lord we are all the same, and had laughed, a strange, rather nervous laugh, and then they'd all gone in the sauna together. Kathrine had wrapped up in her towel, but when she went out to shower, Thomas's father had come out straight after and had stood outside the shower until she was done. He had held the towel out for her, but she had grabbed it out of his hands, and quickly brushed past him, draping the towel round her hips. She felt certain he was watching her.

Nothing in Creation is hidden from His eyes, Thomas's father said later, when they were sitting in the sweating room, everything lies bare and open to the eyes of the One to whom we owe an account of ourselves and a reply. He laughed, and with the palm of his hand brushed some drops of sweat off his chest and belly, so that they flew across the room, and some landed on Kathrine's neck.

Afterward they drank tea, and Thomas's father said, now you're one of us, welcome to the bosom of the family.

Kathrine's girlfriends had congratulated her on their engagement, and her mother was happier than she'd been for a long time. She had liked Thomas right away, had permitted herself to be dazzled by him, just as Kathrine herself had been dazzled by him in the early days. He was good-looking, and was always in a good mood. He had been all over the world, and had an interesting job and a good salary. At first, Kathrine used to ask herself what she had done to find such a husband, and what he saw in her.

Thomas had one of the highest grades in his year, and had a PhD in economics. He had been a champion swimmer as a boy, and had friends on every continent. He could speak five languages fluently, and had once had an offer to be the personal adviser to a cabinet minister in Oslo. He had devised a well-known computer game, and was a black belt in quite a rare form of martial arts. Twice a week he would run the ten kilometers to the airport and back. He had spent a few winters as a substitute skiing teacher in north Norway. Once, he'd gone on a tour with Crown Prince Hakon, and once spent the night in a ski hut on the Hardingervidda with Agnetha from ABBA. And not a word of it was true.

But for Morten, Kathrine would probably never have found out. Morten was her oldest friend, her only real friend. They had known each other since school. Both of them said they'd known each other forever. At the time, everyone thought they would get together sometime, but then Kathrine had got the baby from Helge, and after the divorce, either she or else Morten had always been in a relationship, or some sort of affair. They had always missed each other, as they said from time to time when they had a beer or a coffee together. And Morten and Kathrine would have been a good-looking couple. He was dark, not too tall, and slender. As a child, he had always claimed to have a French grandmother. It wasn't actually the case, but because of that, and because he always kissed girls on both cheeks, they later all called him the Frenchman. Kathrine was pretty sure he had some Sami in him, as many in the village did. Norwegian, Swedish, Finnish, and Sami stock were all mixed together here, in some families there was also Russian or Chukchi. The borders had always been permeable, as the humans simply followed the reindeer herds, the fish migrations, which weren't governed by boundaries. They came to the village because they wanted to work here for a couple of years, because the fish factory paid good money. It didn't matter where you lived, it was cold all over and dark. It doesn't matter, said Morten, I've lost touch with my family anyway.

Kathrine and Morten saw each other often in the village, but after Kathrine married Thomas they never went out together. Thomas didn't want Kathrine to be seen with other men. Not that he didn't trust her, he said, but the village wasn't the biggest, and he didn't want his wife and his marriage to be the subject of gossip.

"And least of all with the Frenchman."

"Why do you call him that? You don't even know him."

"I've known plenty of French men," grinned Thomas, "and plenty of French women, too."

Then, two weeks ago, Morten and Kathrine happened to bump into each other. Thomas and Kathrine and the boy had spent New Year with Einar and Veronica in Tromso. Thomas had taken a couple of days off work to go skiing with Einar. Kathrine flew back on New Year's Day, because she had to work, and the boy had to go to school. That evening, she popped into the Elvekrog.

For weeks and weeks it had been dark. Kathrine had never managed to get used to the darkness of winter, even though she had never known it any other way. In summer, she drew the light into herself, in winter she had the feeling she wasn't alive, or just half-alive, and dreaming. When the sun shone, everything sparkled in its light, and was living and beautiful. Winter was just a long period of waiting.

The bar was almost empty, only the Senegalese physiotherapist from the clinic was there as usual, drinking one beer after another. The floor was littered with rubbish from the New Year's party the night before, with bits of paper chains and little colored cotton wool balls. Kathrine sat at a table in the corner and drank a beer. Then, just as she was about to go, in came Morten, and she stayed.

Morten got two beers at the bar and joined Kathrine. He had recently broken up with his girlfriend, and was quickly on to the subject of love. Kathrine was already a bit tipsy, and over her third beer she was telling Morten that Thomas hadn't slept with her now for almost a year. She knew that was a betrayal of Thomas, and she felt bad about it, and perhaps that was why she went on to tell Morten all about Thomas's excuses, and that she suspected him of betraying her with one of the girls at the fish factory. She told how on their wedding night they had played with each other, as Thomas had referred to it, and when Morten asked what that was about, she told him.

"What did you marry him for?" he asked.

Then Kathrine called her mother, and asked her to keep the boy overnight. Where are you, asked her mother. Nowhere, said Kathrine.

Later, Morten made a sort of declaration of love to her. They had both had quite a bit to drink, and it was past midnight. Morten asked if she fancied going back with him, and Kathrine said yes. He lived right up at the top of the village. They parted outside the Elvekrog, and took different routes, so that no one would see them together. As Kathrine came to the house she lived in, she almost went in. But then she walked past it.

Morten came to the door. He was smiling. He held a bottle of wine in his hand. Kathrine went in. She took the bottle of wine out of his hand, set it down on the table, and kissed Morten on the mouth. They threw their arms around each other, and undressed each other. They went into the bedroom without letting go. Morten went in backward, then he thought he would carry Kathrine in, and he almost fell over in the process. She laughed because he was so awkward. He kissed her to stifle her laughter. Then they were both laughing and kissing and embracing. They made love, and lay together on the bed.

Kathrine lay on Morten. She sat up and looked at him. She took his hands and kissed them.

"*Faire l'amour*," said Morten. Both said they had wanted it for a long time, ever since they could remember even, but Kathrine wasn't sure that was true. She was a little embarrassed to see Morten naked after knowing him for so many years. Once, when he was holding her from behind, she whispered to him to talk dirty to her. He did his best, but he wasn't altogether successful, but that didn't matter either.

"You're not much of a Frenchman, are you," she said. Then she cried a bit because she had a bad conscience. And when he asked her why, she said it was because she loved Thomas. And she wasn't sure it wasn't true.

"Was I good?" she asked later.

"Sweet Kathrine," said Morten. "It's not your fault."

In the morning, Kathrine felt ashamed of what had happened, and she couldn't believe she had asked Morten to talk dirty to her. But he was very nice to her again. In the bathroom, he kissed her on the neck, and that made her cry a little bit more.

She was already dressed. He was standing in his boxer shorts, making coffee. He was singing to himself, and she suddenly felt quite happy and thought she was quite justified in sleeping with him. They parted as friends, without any bad conscience, and without arranging anything for the future. Kathrine was careful not to let anyone see her leave the apartment. In the office, she was still thinking about Morten, because it had been a nice night.

That evening she spent at her mother's, and the following evening Thomas was back. He asked her what she had done while he'd been away. She said, not much, she had been tired still after the holiday. They sat in the living room, Thomas watched television, Kathrine read a book. He asked her if she had gone to bed early, and not stayed up reading, and she said, yes, very early, and smiled. Then she said how she had spent yesterday at her mother's, and what they'd talked about, that they'd gone for a walk, what her mother had made to eat. She looked at Thomas. He wasn't listening. He was sitting quietly on the sofa, and from the side, he looked older than he really was. He would never ask her again about those two days, that evening and that night, she thought, and that's how simple it was. She was astonished how easy she had found it to lie to him, but she didn't feel guilty. She wondered too whether Thomas had lied to her, ever. Once, Veronica had talked about Einar having gone on a ski tour with Prince Hakon as a substitute ski teacher. That's funny, said Kathrine, Thomas did the same thing. Then Veronica had changed the subject, and Kathrine hadn't thought about it anymore. Now she wondered whether Thomas had made up the story, or stolen Einar's story. Or whether Einar had lied. Or both of them.

She asked Thomas about his ski tour with the Crown Prince. He made an evasive reply, and finally asked with some irritation, when she didn't let go of the matter, whether she doubted him.

"What's the name of the computer game you devised?" asked Kathrine. "And what are the languages you speak? Say something to me in French."

Soon after, Kathrine went up to bed. She heard the sound of the television for some time after that, the excited host on a sports show. Norway had won a couple of medals.

The next day, she called Morten and arranged to have lunch with him in the fishermen's refuge. She told him the story of the ski teachers, and Morten thought it could be true. The Prince did ski, and celebrities often took ski teachers with them, when they went on long trips. When she told him about Thomas's black belt, he thought Thomas didn't look that type, and when she said he'd been a champion swimmer when he was a boy, Morten said that should be easy enough to check. They kissed each other good-bye on the cheek, as ever, but this time Morten put his hand on Kathrine's hip, and stroked her briefly. That afternoon, he called her in the office and said Thomas had never been a champion swimmer. And the martial arts school he claimed to have attended in Tromso had no record of his name. And he didn't have a doctorate either.

Kathrine thought about the many inconsistencies she had noticed in Thomas's stories, for which she had never asked him to account, for which he had never offered to give her an account. In the days to come, she researched all she could, and checked every available detail of Thomas's stories. And everything was a lie, everything was made up.

On one of his running evenings, Kathrine followed Thomas. He ran along the main street. There had been a lot of snow that winter, and it lay in deep drifts. She followed him on her bicycle. She was afraid he might spot her, but he never looked round, he jogged on and seemed to be perfectly relaxed.

Just back of the village, where the airfield used to be, Thomas went off the road and ran across the broad field. His parents had a little hut up there, like many of the village families, either here or somewhere else on the fjeld, and that was where Thomas was making for. Kathrine watched, and saw him disappear into the hut. She left her bicycle by the side of the road. A track made by many footprints led across the snow. When Kathrine approached the hut, she walked very slowly and cautiously. She couldn't hear anything. There was light in the windows, and she looked inside, and saw Thomas sitting at the table on his own. He sat there motionlessly in his tracksuit, staring into space. Kathrine put her head down, waited, looked in at the window again. Thomas was sitting there, just like before. Then he got up, put some wood in the stove, got a beer out of a crate in the corner, and sat down again.

The hut was furnished with old furniture that had been replaced in the family house and had been brought out here. They were used pieces from the 1970s, and the curtains were old and faded as well. There were black-and-white photographs on the walls, earlier generations of

Thomas's family. Serious-looking individuals in dark clothing, ships, the carcass of a whale on the ramp of an old port. Beside the doorway was an embroidered verse from the Bible. "Go ye home to the Lord, thy God, and hearken to His voice!"

Thomas sat there motionlessly. Kathrine shivered. She was bored. Half an hour later, Thomas was still sitting there, forty-five minutes, still. She returned to the road. When she reached her bicycle, she cast one more look back at the hut. After a while, the door opened, and Thomas stepped out into the snow. Kathrine pedaled quickly home.

She was only just back when a good-humored Thomas came in, saying he'd taken two minutes less than last time. Then he said he wouldn't mind doing more sports, and he missed the contests. He told her about some of his triumphs, grabbed Kathrine's forearms, and demonstrated a couple of grips. He didn't even notice how cold her arms were. He laughed and said that when he'd left Tromso, he'd been the best fighter in the club. Then Kathrine said, you smell of beer, and I know you didn't run to the airport.

She had followed him, she said, and he said, why, didn't she trust him, and surely he could drink a beer without having to ask for permission. That wasn't the point, Kathrine said, he had lied to her, he had been lying to her all along. But Thomas claimed he had only gone to the hut to check up on things there, his father had asked him to take a look at the stove, which wasn't drawing properly. And when Kathrine drew up a list of his other lies, he replied with fresh claims, and she was convinced he was lying to her. He made wild claims, contradicted himself, his whole life story got mixed up. First he was furious, then he got quieter and quieter, but he didn't give up. When Kathrine said she was leaving, all he said was that she would see he hadn't lied, it was all a conspiracy, he had some powerful enemies. She said he was crazy, and she left.

She went to Morten's, but he wasn't home. She went to the Elvekrog and drank a beer. Then she went to the fishermen's refuge. Svanhild in her dressing gown answered the door. Kathrine apologized, but Svanhild said that was fine, she'd only been watching television. Kathrine said she needed a room. She was crying. Svanhild didn't ask any questions. She got a key, and took Kathrine downstairs to the lower ground floor. She wished her a good night, and lightly brushed her arm with her hand. You're all cold, she said, and she smiled.

Kathrine spent a week in the fishermen's refuge.

Kathrine hardly went out on the street anymore since moving back to her apartment. She didn't go to work, and she only left the house in order to buy necessities. The child often spent the night with his grandmother. He didn't like coming home, now that Thomas wasn't there. He said he'd rather be with his grandmother because he was allowed to bring friends back and his grandmother was a better cook. Kathrine didn't mind. She sat in the apartment, reading or watching television. On one of the days when the sun didn't yet reach the village, but the mountaintops were bathed in light for a few minutes, Kathrine took her skis, and went out to the lighthouse, and talked to the lighthouse keepers.

When she got back late in the afternoon of the following day, she found a moving van in front of the house. She saw Thomas and Einar carrying furniture and cardboard boxes out into the street. She saw Thomas's parents, and Veronica, also helping. She heard them laughing. The engine of the van was running. Kathrine waited and watched from a distance. She was surprised to see Veronica and Einar in the village, then she remembered that tomorrow was Thomas's birthday. When the van had left, she went to the house. There was a letter from the bank in the mailbox, a statement. The customs and excise office had paid her her entire salary, even though she hadn't been in since the middle of the month. Kathrine smiled. She walked up the stairs and let herself into the apartment. It was bare.

You might at least have tidied up after yourself, thought Kathrine. The state of the kitchen. Tidying up is half of life. She walked around the empty apartment. Where the bookshelf had stood there were now two piles of books on the floor, Kathrine's children's books, which she had saved for the boy, and a few American thrillers she had ordered from Tromso. That to her was America. Dark crime-ridden cities. Rainy streets with a few lonely people on them.

In the bedroom, some of her clothes were lying on the dusty floor. Her uniform. So Thomas didn't know she wasn't going to work anymore. You could at least have vacuumed, she thought. In the bathroom, in the little cabinet behind the mirror, were her toiletries. Kathrine looked at herself in the mirror. She put on some lipstick, which Thomas had given her once and she'd never used. Kathrine, she thought, funny name.

In the kitchen were a few gadgets she had bought and that Thomas had always thought were superfluous: a juice press, a grain mill, a rice cooker that had been used only once. The electric wok was gone. I thought that belonged to me, thought Kathrine, and forced a smile.

On the sideboard, there was a note from Thomas. He wrote that he had forgiven her. The apartment was ready, and he was expecting her. He wrote that he had picked up the boy at her mother's. Kathrine had been puzzled to find only some of her things left there. Now she understood. This was another stage of the selection process. Once again, he had pulled out those things he didn't care for, her old dresses, her kitchen things, her books. Her uniform. Why do you work? he had often asked. I earn enough for the three of us.

Kathrine went from room to room. She didn't miss Thomas's things, she had never liked them. She just missed the television. Thomas had left her laptop behind. And the old clock radio, which she had bought with the first money she had earned. At fourteen, she had spent a summer filling shelves at Rimi's, while the other children had gone on holiday with their parents. Thomas had long wanted to throw away the clock radio, he had an alarm with a CD player that was much better. You could choose some favorite music to wake you up in the morning. Only Kathrine didn't have any favorite music.

She switched on the clock radio. The music sounded strangely echoey in the empty rooms. Time to get up, she said, or you'll be late to work. Early bird gets the worm. She sat down on the floor. Not a lot, my life, she thought, there's not much to show for it. She cried. She lay on her belly on the floor and sobbed long and loud. Then she got up. She wiped away the tears and the lipstick, and brushed the dust off her clothes. She went into the bedroom. She took down her old red suitcase, and packed a few clothes into it, and her father's old camera, which he had loved but hardly ever used. The telephone rang. She went into the kitchen and at the bottom of Thomas's note, she wrote: "You won't find me."

She left the house. At the ATM machine, she drew out most of her money, and then she went down to the harbor. She was there at half past eight. The Hurtig Line vessel was due in half an hour. Kathrine was afraid Thomas might go to the apartment, see his note, start looking for her, and come down to the harbor. But he didn't come.

Presumably, he was eating with his family. Presumably, he expected her to turn up.

Kathrine sat in the waiting room. She got up, paced back and forth. She read the graffiti scratched in the varnish of the door frame, telephone numbers, declarations of love, obscenities. In the angle of the door frame, a black felt-tip pen had written: "Arwen and Sean came here in a rainstorm at 8.30 p.m., lost and in love." Kathrine rubbed at it until the writing had disappeared, and her fingertips were warm with friction, and black. Then she cried again, not as hard as before, but quietly and in despair. As the ship drew in, she wiped away her tears.

Thomas and Kathrine. Lost and in love. No, she thought. She had believed Thomas loved her, but he had hardly even been aware of her. She was a good listener. The part she played in his life could have been played by pretty well anyone. But why was he out to impress her? She was inferior to him in every respect. Why did he continually have to rattle on about his feats, his adventures, his achievements? All the things he had told her. And what had she ever told him? He had never asked about anything in her life, and if she did happen to talk about it, he hadn't paid any attention. So she had ended up keeping her stories to herself. Her stories.

She remembered reading once about how the dinosaurs had become extinct because the earth had been hit by a comet. She was still upset about that weeks later, had woken up in the night and gone over to the window to look up at the sky. Later, there was a time she wanted the earth to be struck by a comet. But it didn't happen. On Svalbard, they had found dinosaur prints.

A year ago, the entire staff of the customs and excise office had been flown out onto a ship by helicopter. The flight had been a lovely experience. Kathrine had seen the village from above, and then they had been winched down onto the ship's deck in a basket, and, together with Coast Guard people, they had combed the whole ship. They hadn't found anything. One of the Russian agents had tipped them off, but presumably it was just his way of settling a personal score. Things went on among the Russians that none of the customs people really could understand.

And other than that? She had never been anywhere. She hadn't seen anything, and she had nothing she could talk about. Once, as a little girl, she had stowed away on one of the Hurtig Line ships, along with Morten. They had got as far as Mehamn, five hours away, and then they had been discovered by a crewman, or else they had given themselves up because they were bored, or cold, or hungry, down in the hold.

But was that really what happened? Her mother told the story over and over. How the Mehamn harbormaster had called them to him, and given them something to eat, and put them on another ship the next morning. The local paper had run a report, two young stowaways. Her mother had cut out the article and saved it with the family photographs. Now you've been in the newspaper, she had said.

And what about Helge and the baby? Once the baby was there, there was no point in asking herself how it could have come to that. What was done was done. That was what her father had always said to her mother, what's done is done. When he had to sell his boat, either because the fishing grounds were almost fished out, or the price of fish was going down, or because he was ill or not a good fisherman, who could say. When he went to work in the fish factory, not difficult work, but he was already sick. And when Kathrine went to visit him in the factory, she was about fourteen, and asked him, isn't it boring to do the same thing all day long, he would say what's done is done. As if it didn't matter that he had once owned a boat. But it wasn't true. In the village, nothing was ever done.

Kathrine had sworn to herself that she would never work in the fish factory. That was later, when she was hardly speaking to her father, when he was drinking, drinking more and more. Never the fish factory.

She sat in the German fortifications with Morten. It was cold, they were sitting there in wintertime, and they both swore, never the fish factory. They made plans, travel plans, plans for a life. Their plans were more real than their life. Morten went away. He went to Tromso to work, he went round the world. Two years later, he was back, it was as though he'd never left. He took a job in the fish factory, a desk job, that was something else. And later on, he got a job with the council, he was responsible for the village's home page, and the little radio station that transmitted for an hour or two each day. News, weather reports, the hour for the migrant workers, the phone-in. We congratulate Peder Pedersen on his sixtieth birthday. The male voice choir from Berlevag will now sing. And Kathrine went to work for the customs. Training in Tromso, three stints of three months, the best time of her life.

I could get myself transferred, thought Kathrine. Start a new life. She could have gotten herself transferred, but she never did. And somehow the time had passed, she had hardly been aware of it. One village or another. Earlier, there had at least been a cinema. Now there were just bingo evenings.

Slowly the lights of the village slipped by. The night wasn't cold, but there was a stiff wind. Even so, Kathrine went outside, once the village could no longer be seen from the panorama deck. The further the ship steamed on its course, the larger the village seemed to become. Then it slowly disappeared behind a spit of land, and there was only the orange reflection of its lights visible in the clouds. It got lighter, and for a little while it almost looked as though an artificial sun were rising behind the rocks. The sea swell got stronger, and as Kathrine went inside, she saw a couple of seabirds flying low over the water into the beam of the searchlights and then straight back into the dark again. Snowy rocks glimmered on either side of the fjord. And then the ship was out on the open sea.

When the *Polarlys* docked in Hammerfest the next day, there was already the first hint of light in the sky. The layover was an hour and a half, and Kathrine left the ship to become a member of the Polar Bear Club. She had twice been to Hammerfest before, once with her father and once with Thomas, and each time she had wanted to join, but first her father, and then Thomas had said that was just nonsense and a waste of money. In the clubhouse, she paid her subscription, and was given a postcard, and a polar bear brooch in mother-of-pearl. Elvis had once wanted to join the Polar Bear Club, but they hadn't taken him. You had to apply in person. Elvis Rex. Kathrine had had to laugh, each time she saw the sign in the CD shop in Tromso. She went back on board, and for a while she felt happy and cheerful.

The next morning, she inspected the bridge, along with three German couples. A steward had asked her at lunch the previous day whether she would like to have a look at the bridge and the engine room. The usual program. He had asked how far she was traveling, and Kathrine had said as far as Bergen. Four days yet, said the steward, good, welcome on board the *Polarlys*.

The bridge didn't really interest Kathrine, but she felt lonely on the ship. The captain wore a fine uniform. He had a short reddish beard and lots of burst blood vessels on his cheeks, but he gave Kathrine a friendly smile. He didn't talk much, and when one of the Germans, an old man in a sailor's peaked cap, started talking in English about his war experiences, and how they had used the fjords to hide their submarines, he talked still less. The Germans had big binoculars, and after a while they started talking among themselves in German, and Kathrine didn't understand what they were saying. She stood next to the captain, and from time to time he would hold the back of his hand against the horizon, and gesture, and say, seals, or rocks, or Risoyhamn at last. When Kathrine was the last person to leave the bridge, the captain shook hands with her and said she was welcome back at any time.

The *Polarlys* made two stops in the Lofotens. They crossed the Arctic Circle on schedule the next morning.

The captain refused to believe Kathrine when she said she had never been south of the Arctic Circle before. She had climbed up to the bridge again. They hadn't had any money, she said, her father had worked in the fish factory, and if they went on holiday at all, they didn't go any further than Kiruna. That was where her parents came from. The captain asked her if she was a Sami. Half, she said, through my father. She had attended the customs school in Tromso, and at twenty she had had a baby, and that meant holidays were out of the question. She was pleased she had been allowed to complete the course. Once, a couple of years ago, she had booked a week on Majorca, but then the boy had been ill, and she hadn't gone. She still had to pay for it, though.

"If the child had died," the man at the travel agent's said, ". . . It's funny. I've been watching the borders for years. But I've hardly ever been on the other side. Sweden, Finland, yes, but that's all . . . never even been to Murmansk. I had a friend from there, but I never visited him. A sea captain, like you."

"Things don't look any different on the other side," said the captain, and Kathrine said she knew. Then the captain asked her to have a coffee with him. They went down to the dining room together, which was almost deserted at that hour. A steward was just setting the tables for lunch.

The captain said Kathrine's crossing the Arctic Circle for the first time was something to celebrate. "Welcome to the world," he said, and she laughed. When he asked her where she was going, and whether she was on holiday, she said she didn't know, and no, she was just leaving.

"My honeymoon," she said, and laughed. She took photographs of the captain, and he laughed as well, and wanted to take one of her, but she refused. The captain's name was Harald, and he lived in Bergen.

"If you want," he offered, "you can stay with me for a few days."

Harald lived in a small wooden house painted yellow. His wife had gone to Oslo for a few days with a friend. Harald wanted Kathrine to sleep in their bed. He said he'd be happy with the nursery, he didn't mind. But she refused. He showed her the nursery, and said that his son, whose name was also Harald, had died three years ago in a sports accident. Kathrine was surprised by the term *sports accident*, and asked him what had happened.

"It was while climbing. He fell. He was alone. The fall needn't have been fatal. But he was alone."

Harald looked much younger out of uniform. The rocks were bad here, he said, they weren't solid. A piece of rock had broken off, and buried his son under it.

"He was eighteen. He didn't miss anything. He did what he wanted. As for the girls . . ."

"I'm twenty-eight," said Kathrine, "I don't know if I've missed anything or not. What about you?"

"Forty-five."

"Did you invite me because you knew your wife was away?"

"I wouldn't have asked you if she'd been here."

Harald laughed. He said he had to run a couple of errands in town. He gave Kathrine a key, and asked her if she'd be in for supper.

When Harald had gone out, Kathrine looked around the house. There was a picture of the family hanging in the hallway. The mother looked nice, the boy looked like her. The nursery no longer contained any traces of his having been there, no children's books, no toys, nothing. It was a bright, clean room, and there were pictures on the walls that were like the pictures in hotel rooms, prints of watercolors, scenes from life in the South somewhere. Kathrine took some pictures of the empty room, she didn't know why, and she thought, I shouldn't be doing this.

Then she went into the kitchen to make coffee. She waited for the water to trickle through the filter. A door led from the kitchen to the garage, where there were a couple of bicycles, an ancient Volvo, and a Deepfreeze. Up on one wall were some dusty ropes and climbing harness, and a couple of battered-looking synthetic helmets. When Harald came back from town, Kathrine asked him if he did any climbing himself.

"Not anymore," he said.

"Have you gone on climbing expeditions?"

"Sometimes." Harald shrugged his shoulders. "We got along well. But he was a daredevil. I didn't have any time that day. He went off by himself."

"Did you not want to keep anything of his? Nothing?"

"What are we supposed to keep? His clothes? His books? It's him I miss, not his things."

Harald cooked for Kathrine. He opened a bottle of wine. It was a good evening. Harald talked about his voyages along the coastline, about the spring storms, and the tourists. In his younger days, he'd worked on container ships all over the world. He talked about exotic countries. When he asked Kathrine if she wouldn't like to see Hong Kong or Singapore for herself, she wasn't sure. "All those people," she said. "And I bet there are bugs."

"What about your mosquitoes?" said Harald, and laughed. "At least cockroaches don't sting."

"And did you have a girl in every port?"

"Well, it wasn't like the Norwegian coastal line, that's for sure," said Harald. "Or would you go for a sailor?"

"We have a seamen's mission. Do you know Svanhild?"

Kathrine laughed. She couldn't imagine Svanhild as a sailor's girl.

"I know one or two who'd have been happy with her," said Harald, laughing as well. "She's not the world's greatest cook, but she can run a household when the man's not there. She's competent. And she has a kind heart."

"You're talking like an old fisherman. Like my first husband. Is your wife competent?"

"Very. Our marriage works best when I'm away. Then she can do whatever she wants."

"And when you're there, then she does whatever you want, is that it?"

"Then I do what she wants. She keeps an eye on me. Makes sure I don't drink and smoke too much, or chase the girls."

"So that's what you like to do."

Harald laughed, and then he stopped laughing.

"It works," he said, and he finished his glass. "It's all I can ask for. I know she's got someone else."

When Kathrine didn't say anything, Harald went on: "She's got a man she talks to. An analyst, a shrink, if you like. She sees him in the evenings too, how do I know what goes on there, I'm away all the time."

Still, Kathrine didn't say anything. Harald got a bottle of akvavit from the fridge, and a couple of glasses. He poured.

"I never asked her," he said. "When Harald died . . . But why am I telling you all this?"

"Why are you telling me?" asked Kathrine. She said she was tired, and was going to bed.

When she was in the bathroom, Harald knocked on the door. She was in the shower, she shouted back. Then through the frosted glass of the shower cabinet, she saw that he'd come in. He moved about slowly and carefully. Finally he stopped. Kathrine saw him the way he must see her. She turned round, and turned the water off. Then she heard his cracked voice very close to her.

"I brought you a towel. I'm going out now."

"OK," she said, "thank you."

When she emerged from the bathroom, he was sitting on the floor beside the door. He was pale, but there were little spots of red on his cheeks. He was smoking a cigarette. A column of ash fell off, and he brushed it nervously into the carpet.

"Thank you for taking me in," said Kathrine, "I don't know what else I would have done."

Harald shook his head. "That's how far gone I am. Using my dead son to try and get a woman . . ."

"Be quiet," said Kathrine.

"What else have I got to offer?" said Harald. "My suffering."

"I liked you the moment I saw you," said Kathrine, "when we were on the bridge, and you pointed out that seal."

Kathrine spent two days and two nights at Harald's. On the afternoon of the third day, she took the train to Oslo. At the station, Harald asked her where she was going next.

"I've got a friend called Christian," she said. "He's Danish, lives in Aarhus. I'm going to visit him there."

"Write to me," said Harald. "And when you're next in Bergen . . . stay with me anytime you like. With us. I'll tell my wife about you."

The journey from Bergen to Oslo took seven hours. The train went over innumerable bridges, through tunnels and narrow valleys, past fjords and glaciers. In Oslo, Kathrine got on the night train. She dozed in her seat, she couldn't sleep properly. When she changed trains in Malmo, she was dead tired. Eighteen hours after leaving Bergen, she finally arrived in Aarhus. She took a bus, and rode out to Christian's address. She was surprised to find herself in front of a single concrete apartment block.

Christian's name wasn't next to any of the apartments, but there was a family called Nygard who were listed. A. and K. Nygard. A man just leaving the building held the door open for Kathrine, and she took the elevator up to the fifth floor. From the elevator column, a glass door led to a long narrow corridor off which the apartments opened. Kathrine looked down at the town. She was surprised how flat and monotonous it all looked. The streets were all alike, the houses, the colors. She saw a mailman going from house to house, cars stopping at traffic lights, and then driving on.

There was a straw star hanging on the door of A. and K. Nygard's apartment, even though Christmas was more than a month ago. Kathrine rang the bell. A woman of about fifty in a stylish dress opened the door. Something about her face reminded Kathrine of Christian, perhaps it was the watery eyes, perhaps the soft, undefined features. The woman looked at Kathrine without saying anything. Kathrine asked if a Christian Nygard lived here.

"He's not here," said the woman.

Kathrine asked when Christian was expected back, and the woman said she didn't know, he was installing some machinery in France.

"I thought he was back from there."

"We thought he would be too. But there was some problem. Something technical. He wasn't even able to be home for Christmas."

The woman asked who she was, and when Kathrine said a friend of Christian's, the woman looked at her suspiciously and said Christian had never mentioned her.

"We wrote each other e-mails."

"The Internet has a lot to answer for," said the woman, shaking her head. "I keep telling Christian he needs to get out, and not spend all his time in front of the screen. That Internet's full of the most . . ."

She gestured dismissively. A small, gray-haired man poked his head out into the passage, and eyed Kathrine curiously. Then he disappeared again.

"I'm sorry I can't help you," said the woman.

"Have you got his address?"

"I don't know if I should give it to you. If Christian hasn't given it to you himself . . ."

The woman told Kathrine to wait. She shut the apartment door. After a while it opened again, and the woman handed Kathrine a scrap of paper with the name of a hotel in Boulogne written on it in old-fashioned writing, the Hotel du Vieux Matelot.

"That's the Old Sailor Hotel," said Christian's mother, and she gave a high-pitched, somewhat artificial laugh. Kathrine thanked her, and left.

Five hours after arriving in Aarhus, she was on a train again. She had wanted to have a look at the town, but all the people on the streets had been too much for her, and finally she had taken refuge in a museum that was full of old runestones. She looked at them, but she felt restless, and by the time she was sitting in the train, she had almost no recollection of what she'd seen.

Kathrine felt disappointed. So many years she had been dreaming of a trip to the South. She had supposed that everything would be different south of the Arctic Circle. She had pictured worlds to herself, wonderful, colorful worlds full of strange animals and people as in the books of Jules Verne she had liked so much as a child. *Around the World in Eighty Days, Journey to the Center of the Earth, 20,000 Leagues Under the Sea.* But this world wasn't so very different from the world of home. Everything was bigger and noisier, there were more people around, more cars on the streets. But she had hardly seen anything that she hadn't seen at home or in Tromso. There's not a lot of room in a person, she thought.

In Hamburg, it was raining. There was an hour until the night train for Paris was due to depart. Kathrine stayed in the station, sat down at a table by one of the snack carts. She counted up her money, and thought about the way her mother had forever been counting her money, when they were still living in Sweden, and dreaming of having a fishing boat. Kathrine looked about her suspiciously, before she put the money back in her purse. In one corner sat a family from somewhere in Asia, with lots of luggage and quiet, well-behaved children.

A drunk sat down next to Kathrine and said something to her. While she was in Bergen, she had bought herself an American thriller to read on the train. Now she took it out, opened it at random, and pretended to read. But the man wouldn't leave her alone. He bent forward and looked in her face and said something that Kathrine couldn't make out. Finally, she got up and walked away. The drunk followed her for a few steps, then turned back. Kathrine waited outside in the main hall. By the time her train came in, she was shaking with cold. She was glad there were still empty places in the sleeping cars. She was all alone in her compartment. It reminded her of the cabins on the Russian trawlers, only with a bigger window.

Slowly, the train rolled out of the station. Rain lashed against the window, and Kathrine saw the many lights in the city, and for the first time since setting out she had the feeling of being somewhere out in the wide world.

The train moved through the darkness, with only occasional clusters of lights. Kathrine undressed and placed her clothes on the suitcase, which she had stowed on the middle bunk. She lay down. The train swayed gently, and the monotonous sounds made her sleepy.

Kathrine was walking through an enormous department store. It was dark, only where she was was somehow lit up. The light stayed with her. There were no other people in the store, but she sensed she was not alone, that she was being watched. She knew she had forgotten something, but she didn't know what. She knew she was dreaming, and at the same time she knew the dream was real, because she was dreaming it. Her shopping cart was empty. She walked through the store, between the long shelves that were like walls. She was frightened, even though she felt nothing could happen to her here, that nothing was real, that she was in a dream. She heard the noise of the train, but the dream didn't stop. She was trapped in it.

Kathrine awoke when the light came on in the compartment. She saw two legs right in front of her face, and she heard the voices of the sleeping-car conductor and a young man. She wanted to speak, to tell the conductor that this compartment was reserved for women, and that there must be some mistake. But she didn't say anything, and even shut her eyes when she noticed him stoop to have a look at her. Then the conductor went out, and the man shut the door and bolted it. He put his bags away and sat down on the bunk facing her, and when he saw her eyes were open, he said hello. "In here is for women," she said in

English. The man shook his head and replied that the compartments were not separated by sex. Then the word *sex* seemed to embarrass him, and he said, men and women.

Kathrine pulled her clothes, which she had beside her on her red suitcase, under her blankets. She was only wearing panties and a T-shirt, and she hoped the man would take one of the bunks over her head. But he remained sitting opposite her, and asked her where she was going, and when she said Paris, whether she knew Paris, and where she came from, and what her name was. He said his was Jurgen.

"Where are we?" asked Kathrine.

"Bremen," said Jurgen. "Paris is beautiful. I'm going to Brussels."

He explained that he was an intern with the European Commission, and when Kathrine said she was from Norway, he asked her lots of questions about fishing regulations, and wanted to know her views on catching whales, and the overfishing of the seas. He seemed to know all about Norway. More than I do, thought Kathrine, he knows more about my own country than I do. She said that where she came from, they didn't hunt whales anymore. Then she said she was on her honeymoon, she didn't know what prompted her to say that. Perhaps because she had been afraid, or perhaps just to get him to stop talking about Norway.

"Where's your husband?" asked Jurgen.

Kathrine hesitated. She really didn't want to talk about her marriage with him, and she said, "He's waiting for me in Paris." She thought, it really doesn't matter what I tell him. And then she wanted to see what it felt like, lying to somebody, and making up a story. Her husband, she said, was a genetic scientist, and was giving a lecture at the University of Paris. And she herself? She was a dancer. She had attained international renown, and had been all over the world. But a couple of years ago, she had given up dancing, and was now living in Oslo with her husband. As stories went, it wasn't very plausible. What was she doing in a second-class compartment, if she was a famous dancer? But Jurgen didn't seem to suspect anything. He was just as stupid as she had been. He beamed, and asked her what places she had been to. She talked about going on tour in Europe, in the U.S., in Japan. And when Jurgen asked her about Japan, she was quite happy to tell him. She had once read a book about Japan. The trip had been fantastic. Every evening, she had had a show in a different city, and in the daytime, she had visited all the different temples and gardens.

"There was one man who used to send me roses every day. He followed us on our entire tour, and saw every performance. He was besotted with me. He was on the board at Sony, a very rich man. He filmed me with a video camera, even though that wasn't allowed. A tiny little thing. A prototype. Not for general sale. He was in charge of developing new products."

She stopped. She didn't enjoy inventing stories. She felt wretched doing it, and she couldn't think of what else she was going to tell Jurgen. She couldn't talk to him if she was lying to him. She felt even more alone than she had felt before Jurgen had come into the compartment, and the more she went on, the more baffled she was by Thomas.

"So what is it exactly that your husband does?" asked Jurgen.

"Look, I've got to go to sleep now," she said. "I've got a hard day ahead of me."

Jurgen took off his pants and shirt. He was wearing light blue underclothes, and he didn't seem at all awkward. Kathrine asked him whether he had sisters. Yes, he said, three sisters, why? He turned round, and made his bed. He scratched his bottom. Kathrine felt reminded of a theology student who had done his internship in the village, she couldn't remember his name now. She smiled. Jurgen lay down. He asked her if she'd like to hear a joke. She asked him how old he was. Nineteen, he said, and she said she was tired, and good night.

Kathrine thought about the theology student. He had spent one winter in the village, and had helped the vicar with the community work. He had organized the church fair. Rune was his name, and he had come from Oslo. For a whole month he'd gone around the village, trying to talk people into making things to sell at the church fair. Kathrine had told him there was no point in such a small village.

"I make something for you to buy, and you make something for me to buy. Where's the sense in that? I might as well make something for myself."

"If you make something, I'll buy it," Rune had replied. But Kathrine hadn't made anything. At most, she made coffee for him, he was slightly in love with her, she had noticed. Perhaps he had said something to that effect too. Then she had met Thomas at the bazaar. And Rune had been sensible, he had known she wouldn't leave the village, and that it was no place for him. And he had left.

Rune had asked Kathrine to go to church, but she had never gone, not then or later. She didn't believe in God. Almost no one in the village believed in God, perhaps not even the vicar, who was a nice man, and did his job same as everyone else.

Only Ian believed in God. Ian was the Scottish priest whom Kathrine sometimes met on the street, who worked as a missionary with the Russian seamen. The first time she had seen him had been on a trawler, and she took him for a Russian. She had looked through his rucksack for contraband, but it was only full of Bibles. Ian belonged to an international organization that had been founded to convert people in the Eastern bloc countries, and was now fighting the spread of radical sects. He had set up a little prayer room on the lower floor of the fishermen's refuge. He asked the seamen along, made them cups of tea, talked and sang and prayed with them, if they wanted. When Kathrine ran into him, he was always in a woolen hat, and with an old rucksack full of Russian Bibles. Then he said how unhappy he was in the village, and how lonely, and she walked with him a bit, and tried to comfort him. She asked him why he didn't get himself posted somewhere else, and said he surely couldn't buy happiness for others at the expense of his own unhappiness. But Ian said Jesus had brought him here, and Jesus would take him away again. She said the Hurtig Line brought you here, and will take you away again.

"The people here believe in God, they just don't believe in Jesus," Ian said once, "they believe in the Creation, but they don't believe in love."

"Well, Creation exists," said Kathrine, "whereas love . . ."

Then Ian said he wished she and her husband could be brought together again. Kathrine said Helge wasn't her husband anymore, and Ian said he would still pray for both of them. And now Thomas wasn't her husband anymore either, and Kathrine wondered whether Ian would pray for them too, and she hoped it wouldn't help. She thought of her son as if he were Thomas's rather than her own.

For the church bazaar, Ian had glued sand and shells onto little picture frames, dozens of little ornamented picture frames, but no one had wanted to buy them. Finally, Rune had bought a couple, and given one to Kathrine. He put a picture of himself in the frame. Kathrine threw away the frame after Thomas had made fun of it. She kept the picture.

When Kathrine woke up, Jurgen was gone. There was a knocking on the door, and then more knocking. She opened it without getting up. It was the sleeping-car conductor. He handed her her ticket back, and her passport, and said they would arrive in Paris in a quarter of an hour, and he wished her an enjoyable stay. Kathrine looked at her watch. The houses outside must already belong to Paris. The train traveled through endless suburbs, past tall, narrow houses, through suburban stations. There were lots of people standing on the platforms, watching as the train rushed through. A few were reading newspapers, a few turned their heads to watch. There must be a Kathrine among them, or a Catherine, with a child and a husband and a lover. Someone who stood there every morning, went to work, made coffee, ate lunch with her colleagues, and went home again.

Kathrine lay on her bunk and looked out the window. Outside, a very crowded commuter train slowly passed them, and the commuters stared across at her, quite unashamedly they stared, in the certainty that nothing would happen to them. Kathrine felt like pulling the blanket up over her head, but instead she stood up and went over to the window, dressed only in her panties and T-shirt. She tried to make the men look at her, but they all lowered their eyes. Only one young man kept looking, their eyes met briefly.

The sleeper slowed down. The other train had now overtaken it, and beyond the tracks, Kathrine could see gigantic warehouses and factories, ugly yellow-white or gray buildings, with the names of companies on them that she had never seen before. The city looked different from the way Kathrine had imagined it, different from Thomas's descriptions of it. But then, this isn't Thomas's Paris, she thought, this is my Paris.

She got dressed, and went to the washroom. She was astonished to see herself in the mirror. When she looked in her eyes, she saw the fear she had almost forgotten she had.

In the metro an old man and a young woman were performing together. The man played an accordion while the woman sang. Kathrine knew they were from Russia, she didn't need to look at the little cardboard sign they had in front of them on the ground, next to a little saucer of money.

She thought about Alexander, who was dead, who was no longer there. If they at least manage to find him, and give him a burial. Even the dead deserved a place. But he was gone, just gone, vanished in the same way as she had vanished. Nothing was where it was supposed to be anymore.

She got on the first metro that arrived. As it drove off, it made sounds like a ship and swayed a little from side to side. Kathrine had sat down on a folding seat. Opposite her was a man in white socks reading a newspaper, who looked at Kathrine over the top of his reading glasses from time to time. She looked out the window. The name of the first station was Poissonniere. *Poisson*, as she remembered, was the word for fish. That's what it said on the boxes at Nils H. Nilsen's. *Filet de Poisson*.

She traveled a couple of stops, and then got off. She walked along tunnels and underground lobbies and found herself—without having seen daylight—in one of the vast department stores Thomas had mentioned to her. But everything was different from the way he had described it. She wondered whether he had lied to her, or she had perhaps deceived herself, not understanding what he was telling her. There must be a colored glass dome in a café somewhere. She took the elevator to the top floor, where the café was. But there wasn't any colored glass dome. The place was very big, with cheap decor, white-painted wooden lattices, and plastic blossoming boughs, which gave it the appearance of a garden café. *Printemps*, Kathrine knew, meant spring. She had never been in a garden café before, but she knew right away what it was, and perhaps for that reason mistrusted it. It looks, she thought, the way a Norwegian who has never seen a garden café might imagine one to look. She smiled. She got herself a coffee, and sat down at one of the tables.

Nearby sat a man of about fifty. He wasn't eating or drinking anything. Beside him he had a sheaf of papers covered with writing. He looked over at Kathrine. She smiled, but he didn't react, and just looked at her for a long time with curiosity. She put her tray back, and took the escalator downstairs. Then she saw the colored glass dome, over the atrium in the middle of the building. It was pretty, but Kathrine had imagined it would be bigger and prettier.

She walked along between counters, as though looking for someone. Everything was much too nice for her. Undergarments were called *lingerie* in French. She took an unbelievably sheer nightie, all trimmed with lace, off a rack, held it in front of herself, and looked at the effect in the mirror. It was a ridiculous sight, the dark blue fleece over her shoulders and the fine, flowing silk. It's so delicate, she thought, I could just stuff it in my pocket and leave with it. But that's not my style. She looked at the price tag. That wasn't her style, either. The whole department store smelled of vanilla.

On the ground floor, she bought herself some perfume. She passed the counters of the various cosmetics firms, the young salesgirls who were no prettier than she was, but much better dressed, and carefully made up. They spoke to the customers, and squirted perfume on their hands, the backs of their hands, their wrists. None of them came up to Kathrine. At one counter, there was a little purple bottle, with the word *Poison* on it in gold. Fish, she thought, what a strange name for a perfume. She held out her hand to one of the salesgirls, who took it between her fingertips, turned it over, and squirted some perfume on her wrist. Kathrine sniffed at it, but she couldn't smell it in the suffocating scent of a thousand other perfumes. She could only smell the alcohol, which slowly evaporated and chilled her wrist. The salesgirl had already turned away. She was talking to a colleague, and Kathrine had the feeling they were both making fun of her, maybe for the suitcase she was carrying around with her. Then she said she wanted a bottle of *Poison*. It was very expensive, but who cared.

She went out on the street. A man walked by, dressed like an orange. Kathrine was relieved when she saw the steps down to the metro. She was relieved that she knew where she was going. She was looking forward to seeing Christian, and hoped he would be pleased at her visit. She was annoyed she hadn't traveled through to Boulogne.

She imagined how Christian would touch her, how he would kiss her neck, push his hand under her fleece, under her T-shirt. He was lying next to her, kissing her, his hands were everywhere, he was whispering in her ear, he was lying on top of her, she sat on him. The room was furnished with beautiful antiques. There was even an open fireplace, with a fire burning. It was warm, and there were lots of blankets and sheets on the bed, and a very soft mattress that squeaked when they moved.

Kathrine took the metro back to the Gare du Nord. The Russian singer and her accompanist, her father or her lover, weren't there anymore, but maybe that was a different tunnel than Kathrine was going through this time, she couldn't be sure.

Dusk was falling as Kathrine arrived in Boulogne. She asked a taxi driver for directions to the Hotel du Vieux Matelot, and then walked there, even though it was raining, and it was a long way. The hotel was an ugly modern building. The door was locked. Kathrine rang. It took a long time for someone to answer, then a young man came along. Before letting her in, he scrutinized her through the glass door. She asked whether Christian Nygard was staying at the hotel. The young man nodded, and asked whether she wanted a room. Yes, she said. The man had her fill out a form, and handed her a key. She asked what Christian's room number was. Seventeen, said the young man, he had put them both on the same floor. But Monsieur didn't get back from work until very late. The room was furnished with old pieces that didn't go together. On the wall there was a color print of Venice. The heating was off, and the room took a long time to get warm, after Kathrine had turned the knob. The view out of the window was of a narrow street. There was no one around at all.

So this was where Christian was staying, and this was his life, these little rooms in hotels, in some town or other. Kathrine wondered what he had in the way of possessions that he took with him, if he had books or pictures from home. Suddenly, she wasn't sure whether it was such a good idea to come. They had liked each other quite well, but maybe there was a woman here whom Christian liked too. A woman who walked through these streets every morning, who had caught his eye, whom he had spoken to in a café or a bar. A customs employee, thought Kathrine, called Chantal or Marianne, with a baby. Unhappy. Christian will meet her, they will drink wine together, he will show her the home page of his company, later on he'll send her e-mails, which will say that the women in Denmark are different from the women in France. She will write back, first in the hope that the episode was more than that, because she will believe she's found at least a friend, and then later on out of habit. Christian won't make her happy, Chantal, or Marianne, or whatever her name is.

Christian was no sort of Don Juan, he hadn't so much as kissed Kathrine. But maybe he just hadn't liked her. Her breasts were on the small side, too small, she thought. And she was too boyish altogether, she hardly had any hips. And she'd rather have been blond. Why didn't she get her hair dyed, Thomas had suggested once, but she didn't want to do that.

Perhaps Christian liked women better who had big breasts and blond hair. Perhaps he liked exuberant women with long, painted fingernails. Women who laughed aloud and had a slinky walk like cats. Maybe French women were different, the way Portuguese women were different. That's what he'd written to her after all, back when he'd been in Portugal. I'm sure, thought Kathrine, that he's got a girl here and a woman there. He'll be annoyed that I showed up. I'll see him at breakfast, she thought, I won't

knock on his door. He can't do anything about me staying here, it's a free country, I can do as I please. But what's
that good for? It got darker in the room. Kathrine didn't
turn the light on. She was incredibly tired, she had never
felt so tired. She lay on the bed, she thought about Thomas,
she thought about her son, her mother, Alexander. It was
as though she was thinking twice over, as though a second stream of thoughts were following the first, that only
occasionally left her with a picture and penetrated her
consciousness, a dark, blurry picture where you couldn't
make out much, a room, people who were doing things
or had done something, some expectation or memory.

She was afraid. She felt she was losing her mind. As if
she were very old and had a life full of enigmatic encoun-
ters behind her, of which she had only a dim memory.
There were hints of dreams, maybe dreams she had once
had, and that now that they were coming at the wrong
time, only frightened her. Stories waiting for their end-
ings. There was something to be done, but she didn't
know what it was. Someone wanted something from her.
People were crowding her. A shadow, which seemed to
be her, was running off ahead, and she couldn't catch up
with it. There was a world waiting for her, just by her,
an incredibly big, dark world, with laws of its own.
Nothing went away. The other figures only moved when
she moved. Just like the game she'd played when she'd
been a child. You had your back turned to the others,
and they ran toward you, and when you turned round,

they stopped still. It was Kathrine's turn, but she didn't dare to turn away. She was afraid the others would jump on her if she turned her back.

She didn't move. She stood by the window and waited, just waited for the figures to disappear. It was cold in the room. Kathrine pulled her uniform out of her suitcase, and put it on. She looked at herself in the mirror, ran her hands over the stout material of the overalls. A customs inspector, she thought, but it didn't help. She took the bedspread off the bed, rolled herself up in it, and lay down on the floor next to the radiator, which was slowly getting warm. She cried silently to herself. She was afraid.

Kathrine didn't know how much time had passed when she heard a knock on the door. She was still lying on the floor next to the heater. It was dark in the window, she could see a slice of sky, but no stars. She heard Christian's voice. Kathrine, he called, are you there? Yes, she called back, I'm coming.

When she saw Christian's shocked expression, she almost had to laugh. She threw herself around his neck and said, I'm so glad you're here. He held her a little awkwardly, gave her little pats on the back, and asked if she was all right. And what she was doing here. And how she had found him. And why she was wearing her uniform. They let go of each other. Kathrine sat down on the bed. Christian switched on the overhead light and shut the door. Then he sat on the bed, a little bit away from Kathrine.

"Your parents told me where you were."

"You saw my parents? Did she let you in?"

"Have you got time for me? I don't want to . . . have you got a girlfriend here?"

"A girl in every town," Christian laughed. "I have so much work to do . . ."

"What time is it?"

"Nine o'clock. Shall we go and eat something? The restaurants close early in winter here."

Kathrine went into the bathroom. She left the door slightly ajar, and talked to Christian while she got changed. He asked her what she felt like eating.

They ate in a bistro near the hotel. It was cold. The waiter pushed a paraffin stove nearer to their table, but it didn't help much. The food was not especially good. The wine warmed Kathrine up, and gradually dispelled her confusion. Christian asked why she'd left, what she'd come here for. And she told him about Thomas's lies, and her flight. She told him how she'd followed Thomas to his parents' hut, and how he'd sat there motionless. That she'd been frightened. She didn't talk about Morten.

"Why does everyone up there have those little huts? What happens in them?"

"They go there on Saturdays," said Kathrine. "They sit at tables, and drink coffee or beer. And on Sunday, they go back home again."

Christian laughed.

"Since I've left, I haven't seen the sun," said Kathrine. "I felt frightened."

"Are you frightened now?"

"I'm not sure. It might come back. I don't know what I'm doing here."

"Fear is the possibility of freedom," said Christian, and he smiled. "How did you like Paris?"

Kathrine said she hadn't seen much of Paris. Christian pulled a yellow envelope out of his briefcase, and took a pile of photographs out of it.

"I was there last weekend," he said. "Do you want to see the pictures I took? I picked them up today."

They looked at the photographs together. The waiter brought coffee, and offered them each a calvados. He filled their glasses up to the brim.

Paris looked the way Kathrine had imagined it, the way she'd seen it in travel brochures and book illustrations. A beautiful city under a blue sky.

"It's beautiful, even when it's raining," said Christian. "You should have seen it."

"What happens now?" asked Kathrine.

"I go home in two days. It took longer than we planned, but we're done now. The final run-through is tomorrow."

He asked if she had enough money, and if she felt like visiting the factory tomorrow, and having a look at the machinery.

"Do you want to meet me for breakfast?" he asked, once they were back at the hotel.

"OK," she said. "Christian . . . ?"

"Yes?"

"I'm not going back."

"I see."

"And thank you. Thank you for dinner."

The fish factory was in a little southern suburb of the city. Kathrine and Christian took the bus. They walked the last bit along the cliffs. The sky was still overcast, but it was starting to clear in the west, and the sea had a white sheen in the sun.

"Has the sun come back where you are?" asked Christian.

"Probably, for a couple of days now," said Kathrine. "Hard to say. It comes back so slowly. You hardly notice."

She hated the darkness, she said.

In the factory, Christian gave her a white coat and a white gauze hood. He waited for her outside the women's locker room. He was in a coat and hood as well.

"It's crazy," said Kathrine. "I come to France for the first time in my life, and I see a fish factory. I haven't even seen the Eiffel Tower."

"You're right, this isn't much different from Nils H. Nilsen's," admitted Christian. "Sorry. I didn't think of that." He pointed to a machine. "A Baader 142 Princess Cut Slaughtering machine."

"I wish you'd saved it to impress your other girlfriends," Kathrine said, laughing.

"If we leave early tomorrow, we can go and see the Eiffel Tower in Paris. Would you like that?"

Kathrine hesitated.

"Sure . . . well, I don't know what your plans are," said Christian.

"What about you? What do you want?"

"I'll be happy to show you the Eiffel Tower," said Christian. They passed long rows of male and female workers who picked the split fish carcasses from the conveyor belt, and trimmed them to filets with a few swift knife strokes, and tossed the pieces on another conveyor belt. Kathrine remembered her father, the way he stood there, slightly hunched forward, his back hurting. He turned around, and threw her a half a fish, which she caught and threw back. That's a nice fish you caught, said her father, and he carried on working. They were paid for piecework.

"But you've seen it all before," said Christian.

Kathrine said she'd go back to town, she wanted to walk on the beach. He said the test run was starting at ten o'clock, it wouldn't take much longer. Actually, the tests had all been done, and this was more by way of a demonstration for the management.

"After that we go for lunch, and drink wine and calvados, and I should be all done by around two o'clock."

He took Kathrine back to the locker room. They arranged to meet back at the hotel in the early afternoon. Kathrine washed her hands, dropped her coat in a blue laundry tub, and left the factory.

She walked back to the main street, and the bus stop. The next bus didn't leave for another half an hour. There was a café by the bus stop, called Aux Travailleurs de la Mer. Two men were sitting, playing lotto. The numbers were flashed up on a screen. Kathrine drank a café au lait, and then she went out. Two children were staring in at the café through the big windows, others were sitting on wooden benches alongside a bumper car, which was not yet or no longer in operation. Kathrine had liked the music in the café, men with gentle voices, singing in French. Everything was gentler here, the language, the voices, the children's games, the weather, the air, which was damp and wrapped itself around her, and the wind that blew in off the sea, and wasn't cold, but still took her breath away.

She wondered how her life might have been different if she'd been born here, and had lived here. Randy would be sitting on a bench beside a bumper car. She would speak French, her name would be Catherine. She would be a better cook maybe, and dye her hair. But I wasn't born here, she thought, so there's no point in even thinking about it. I am as I am, and that's it. For always.

A line of cars emerged from a side street, decorated with white ribbons and flowers. When they had turned onto the main street, they veered about dangerously. The drivers must be drunk, and the people in the cars looked very serious as they passed the bus stop.

Something old, something new, something borrowed, something blue, thought Kathrine. What did I borrow when I married Helge? With Thomas, it was a pearl necklace of Veronica's. And blue? A little blown glass bird that someone had given to her when she was a little girl. And old and new? Thomas didn't get it, he called it all a superstition. The best day of my life, thought Kathrine.

The bus drove up a green hill into the town. On one side of the road was a cemetery, on the other a soccer field. A man who had four blue dots tattooed on the back of his hand and something written on his arm that she couldn't read had sat down in front of Kathrine. She only just got a glimpse of it as the man raised his arm to press the stop button. He got off at the railway station.

Kathrine rode on as far as the sea, and went into the aquarium. "For those who love the sea," it said on a sign outside. There was almost no one there but children with their parents, and she felt rather out of place. She saw jellyfish, sharks, strange spider crabs, enormous red creatures that kept trying to scramble up the black back walls of the aquarium, and kept falling back. There was piano music coming out of loudspeakers. The tuna fish looked very serious, and had ancient faces. There was a dark room that looked like the deck of a trawler. Kathrine read the signs on the walls, which were written in English and French. Another world, and the catch depended entirely on the decisions the skipper took. After God, he is the master of the ship. Kathrine thought about Alexander. He certainly hadn't believed in God. No more than she did herself, or most of the people in the village, no matter what Ian said. Life was too hard where they lived, they didn't have time for things like that. It's a tough job, it said on one sign, life isn't lived by the normal rhythm of day and night, but by the rhythm of the sea and the schools of fish.

At the exit, there was a notice board, where visitors could leave a note of their impressions. "I loved the spider crab because there so big"—a child's writing. Randy would have liked those too, thought Kathrine. At the souvenir shop she bought him a postcard of a spider crab, and a kit for a model trawler, bigger than the *Verchneuralsk*, bigger than Alexander's ship.

The sea was yellow-green and the sky a grayish blue. The wind was blowing hard, and sheets of sand blew past Kathrine's ankles. It was as though the ground was shifting under her feet. She walked along the beach, thinking that it was the same sea that battered the rocks thousands of kilometers to the north, the same sea as the one in which perhaps Alexander had drowned, on which the *Verchneuralsk* continued to fish without him, on which

Harald would soon be under way again, taking his *Polarlys* to the north. It was the sea she had so often sat beside when she'd felt unhappy, and had gone out on the Kongsfjord, and sat on the beach there while the child played. There was still sand in her shoes when she was in Paris.

Kathrine went into Boulogne Cathedral. A choir was rehearsing. She stopped and listened, when a young man walked up and spoke to her. She didn't understand what he wanted. She shook her head, and he went away.

Kathrine had never been inside a Catholic church before. She was impressed by the many candles, by the beautiful Virgin Mary, and the statues everywhere. She lit a candle herself, and put down the suggested money. A candle for what, or to what? For Christian and me, she thought. But Christian was nothing more than friendly. She asked herself what he would have done if she hadn't turned up. He appeared not to have a girlfriend. But maybe he frequented prostitutes. Or he surfed the Web, or got drunk in a bar, or just sat there at a table, like Thomas did in his parents' hut. And waited.

He didn't want anything from her. He wasn't interested in her. Maybe he wasn't interested in women. She had never seen him with one. And now he was friendly, just as he was always friendly, wanting to show her Paris, and then put her on a train that would take her back to Bergen or to Narvik, where she would get on a ship. He would give her a kiss on the cheek, and wish her a good trip and give her money if she asked him for some. And in a few weeks' time he would send her an e-mail from some other country.

What was she thinking? What did she want from him? She wasn't sure if he was more to her than a friendly face in a foreign land. She would have let him kiss her then, when he was in the village, and she didn't have anyone. She would let him kiss her now. She would sleep with him, she wanted to sleep with him. He meant more to her than Thomas did, maybe. But Thomas was her husband, she had made some promises to him, and he had made the same promises to her. He was a liar, but that promise was one he would keep, Kathrine was sure of that. He would never understand her, he would never touch her, but he would give her and her child a home, and would look after them if they were sick. His mother would too, and his father, Veronica, and Einar. They would look after her, they would buy her Christmas presents and birthday presents. Just as Kathrine would buy presents for them. She would.

She left the cathedral. The wind pushed the last of the clouds away to the east. Kathrine took deep breaths of the cold air. She felt as if she could breathe only when it was light. She thought of the Arctic night, those dark months in the village. Then she felt as though she was taking in the air through her skin, as though everything was dissolving and melting into a dark mass. All the people, all the objects, the houses, the snow, and the rocks overlaid one another like shadows and merged into a big, shapeless darkness.

Kathrine went back to the hotel. It was one o'clock. She packed her things, paid for the room, and went to the station. A train had just left. The next one was going in an hour. She sat down in the station café and ordered a beer.

She looked through the high windows and had a view of tower blocks on the other side of the square, a piece of sky, clouds. Before the train came in, Christian appeared in the café. He sat down opposite Kathrine. He didn't speak, just looked at her with a beaming, or a drunken, smile. He ordered a café au lait.

"Café olé," he said, and laughed awkwardly. "I'm a bit drunk, I'm afraid. I don't like to drink in the daytime. But it was a sort of farewell party. The French . . ." He laughed.

Kathrine made a face.

"I didn't want you to come on my account . . ."

"I wouldn't mind going back to Paris," he said when she didn't say any more. "That's true. I don't know when I'd get to see it again."

"And then?"

"Well . . . then I suppose we both go back."

"Thomas emptied out my apartment."

"Is that your second husband?"

She shrugged her shoulders, and told Christian what she hadn't told him before. He didn't say anything, and she wasn't sure whether he was listening to her or whether he was too drunk. When she was finished, she said, "I don't know what to do with myself. I don't have very much money left. Eventually I'll have to go back. To Thomas, I suppose."

"Is it just because of the money?" Christian asked. "Because if you need some . . ."

"Where else would I go? I can't start a new life."

"I sometimes have the feeling my life hasn't even begun," he said. "I'm glad you didn't see my room in Aarhus." He laughed. "I've got a picture of the Danish national soccer team up on the wall. I would have taken it down long ago, if I'd had any idea what I was going to put up in its place."

"But you get around so much."

"That's one possibility. Flight," said Christian, and smiled at her. "Compared to me . . . you've had a baby, you've been married a couple of times. That's a life."

"What about you?"

"I've got a girlfriend in Aarhus. She's a nurse. She goes and sees my parents when I'm not there. She trades recipes with my mother."

He laughed. Kathrine felt sorry for him. She smiled and said, "Shall we go back to the hotel?"

The hotel lobby was dark. On the stairs, Kathrine asked Christian what different places he had been to.

"All over," he said. "Shall I show you the pictures?"

"Have you got them here?"

"Yes," he said, letting himself into his room. "I'll show you."

His room was even smaller than Kathrine's. She sat down on the bed. There was an open suitcase on the floor, a pair of socks soaking in the washbasin. On the tiny table, which—as if to catch its fall—had a TV suspended over it, there was an old Danish newspaper, and a little model fighter plane, almost finished.

"To pass the time," said Christian, "a Messerschmitt Me 109. The fastest plane in the world, in its day. Before the war."

He picked up the model, flew a couple of loops with it round Kathrine's head, and then went on the attack with machine-gun fire.

"Don't do that," she said.

He apologized for the mess in the room. Tidying up is half of life, Kathrine thought, but she didn't want to be thinking about Thomas just now.

"It's your room," she said.

"The less you make yourself at home, the easier it is to leave," he said.

He had got a pile of red and yellow envelopes out of his suitcase. He sat down next to Kathrine, and showed her the photos. He looked at them, one after another, and then passed them to her with a brief introduction, sometimes just a word or two. Most of the pictures were of buildings and landscapes, the sea, a few of the sky, and cloud formations. At the end were pictures of people. A group of men in white coats in front of a fish factory. Sometimes Christian was in the pictures himself. The men stood close together, their arms were around each other's shoulders, someone had cracked a joke, and they were all laughing. Colleagues of mine, said Christian. Portugal, he said, Grimsby, that's in England, Bremerhaven, Holger, he's a friend of mine, Vancouver. "Rome," he said, and he handed Kathrine a picture of him with the pope. "The Holy Father."

"Are you Catholic?"

"Yes," he said. "There's not many of us in Denmark."

"What's it like, being Catholic? I visited the cathedral here."

"I don't know. I've never been anything else. Nice."

There followed more pictures of seaside towns, fish factories, harbors, and ships. A man hoisting two gutted fish aloft, and smiling.

"I follow the fish," said Christian. "Wherever the fish go, so go I."

"Why follow the fish?" asked Kathrine. "There are fish all over."

"They move through the ocean in schools," he said. "I can't imagine it. How far they swim. Whether they know each other. There are so many of them. They multiply."

He said he imagined that fish liked being together.

"If they stay together, they must enjoy each other's company."

Kathrine laughed, and keeled over backward onto the bed. She pushed her shoes off, drew up her feet, and rested her hands on her thighs. Christian turned to look at her.

She smiled, and grinned at him. "What sort of feelings do you have? Or are you a fish?"

"We could leave today," he said. "I'm finished here. If we hurry, there's a direct train to Paris at four o'clock. I know a pretty little hotel there."

They arrived in Paris a little after six. From the Gare du Nord, they went straight to the Trocadero. They crossed the square between the two wings of the Palais de Chaillot. The Eiffel Tower was all lit up and beautiful.

"It looks exactly the way I imagined it," said Kathrine. She bought a little bronze-colored model of it from a pavement dealer, and then got another one for Christian. "Souvenir," she said, and he said, "Are we having a good time?"

"Yes," said Kathrine. "*Oui*. Shall we go up?"

"Do you want to?"

Christian pulled a face, and Kathrine laughed.

"Danes don't have a head for heights. Is that it?"

"The suitcase," claimed Christian.

They took the elevator up to the second platform. That's enough, said Kathrine, as she looked down. She took one picture with Christian in it, and one without. For public and private recollections, she said.

"Now I'll have something to tell people about, too," she said. And suddenly she found herself crying.

"You mustn't feel sorry for yourself," said Christian. "Haven't you got some sort of tower up there, too?"

"The tallest radio mast in Norway," said Kathrine, and wiped her tears away, "but you can't go up it. I've never cried as much as I have this month."

"Any other place you have to have gone to?" asked Christian.

They took a taxi, and drove through the city, down the Champs-Elysées, over the Place Vendôme and past the old and new opera houses. Kathrine took pictures out of the window, and by the time they reached the hotel, the roll of film was finished. The hotel was in a little side street.

"We could share a room," said Kathrine. "That would save money."

"I don't know if they have rooms with twin beds here."

"I don't mind sharing a bed," said Kathrine. That was saying too much and not enough, she thought, while Christian talked with the elegantly dressed, dark-skinned lady at the desk. He tried to talk French. The woman was very patient, but before long she had switched to English.

"If you prefer, we could move another bed into the room."

"No, no, that's OK." Christian blushed, and Kathrine turned away and went over to a stand full of leaflets on various tourist attractions. She took one out about a Village Gaulois, and looked at it. There were pictures of wooden huts, and types who resembled the characters in the Asterix comics she had read when she was little. Kathrine thought about the Sami village at Jukkasjarvi, where her father had worked at the time he met her mother. He had called it the Lapp Zoo, when he'd had to depict the traditional way of life of the Sami for the benefit of tourists. As a little girl, Kathrine had gone there often. Her mother had made a Sami costume for her, and had worn one herself, even though she looked rather strange in it. Her family had traveled up to Kiruna from south Sweden before the war. Kathrine's grandfather and great-grandfather had both worked in the iron mines, enormously strong fair-haired giants. Her mother was blond as well, and looked typically Swedish. Her grandfather, whom Kathrine had never met, was a devout and strict man. When his daughter came home and told him she was getting married and was pregnant, he almost murdered her. And when he learned that the father of her child was a Lapp, he stopped speaking to her. There was no church wedding, her father had threatened the priest, and none of the family members appeared at the registrar's office, in the town hall.

Kathrine had often asked herself how her father had won over his mother, how he had managed to seduce the strictly brought-up girl, who was also fully a head taller than he was. The Sami have more testosterone than the Swedes, her father had said, and laughed. But Mother had said he wanted to buy a fishing boat. "He wanted to get out, and I wanted to get out, too."

The tourists had snapped pictures of Kathrine, the little Lapp girl among the reindeer, and her father had given them a ride once around on the reindeer sleigh. The authentic life of the Sami. After work, they had taken off their costume, and driven home in the old Volvo, to their two-room apartment. Her father had switched on the television, and her mother worked out how much money they still needed for their fishing boat.

The hotel receptionist gave Christian a key. She called him Monsieur and Kathrine Madame.

"Madame," said Christian, unlocking the room.

"I feel like . . . ," she began, and then stopped short.

"Shall we have something to eat?" asked Christian. He said he knew a good restaurant in the area.

They walked for about a quarter of an hour through dimly lit streets, then finally he admitted he had gotten lost. They had to stop three separate people before someone told them the way.

The restaurant was in a dark courtyard. Outside it was a stall with *fruits de mer* in baskets on ice. It was still early, there were not many people there.

"Why don't your people eat shellfish?" Christian asked.

"I don't know," said Kathrine. "I suppose because there's enough fish."

"Do you feel like trying? I'll show you how to eat oysters."

He ordered a plate of *fruits de mer*, and showed her the way to extract the snails from their little houses, and how to get the oysters and the other shellfish off their shells. Kathrine was astonished to think she had never eaten shellfish before, but she didn't especially like it.

"They don't taste of anything," she said.

Christian cracked a lobster claw for her. They drank white wine, ordered a second carafe, and left their water alone. Their hands touched, and once, Christian held out a morsel of lobster to Kathrine on his fork. Then they drank bitter coffee and calvados, and ate ice cream with hot chocolate sauce. The waiter came along with a little copper can, and poured molten chocolate over the ice cream until they called stop. The restaurant was now full. It was hot and noisy. Kathrine felt drunk with the wine and everything else.

That's how you seduce women, she thought, when they were back in the hotel, and Christian was climbing the narrow steps behind her. But he doesn't want to seduce me. She didn't know whether she wanted to seduce him or not. It had been a nice evening, she had hardly thought of Thomas at all, or her son, or her village. Now she was tired, and she even felt a tiny bit sick from so much food and wine.

Madame, your room. Christian disappeared into the bathroom, and Kathrine sat down on the bed. She was afraid of the moment he would emerge from the bathroom. She wondered what he would have on, and what she should wear. Usually she just wore a T-shirt in bed. She took it out of her suitcase. It was a tight, worn old T-shirt, with a faded beer advertisement on it. Macks Ol—the

Most Northerly Brewery in the World. It must date from
her time with Helge, he had probably been given it when
he bought a case of beer once, and given it to her when it
didn't fit him.

Kathrine felt ashamed. She felt ashamed of her T-shirt,
of her entire wardrobe, of her panties, those same practi-
cal panties that she bought in packs of three, and that were
worn by just about all the women in the village, young and
old alike. She felt ashamed of her village, of her stories, of
Helge above all, but also of Thomas, of her mother, and
of the child she hadn't wanted. She felt ashamed of her
apartment, of her books, of not knowing how you tasted
wine, or how you ate shellfish and snails. She felt ashamed
of her whole life. She stuffed the T-shirt back into her
suitcase.

Christian emerged from the bathroom in loose-fitting,
pale-blue-and-white-striped pajamas. He was wearing slippers, and he looked altogether like an English nobleman
in one of the books she had read when she was little. He
should, she thought, have been carrying a candlestick with
a single burning candle in it. Christian smiled, switched
on the bedside light, switched off the main light, and
climbed into bed. She had the feeling that he was moving
terribly slowly, like a figure in a dream.

It was her turn to go to the bathroom. She got undressed,
and looked at herself in the mirror, which was still steamed
around the edges. Considering my age, she thought, and
then, bah, who cares, whatever will be will be. She ran her

hands over her hips, as if to sculpt fresh curves. This is me, she thought, this is my body. That's all there is.

Kathrine washed with a cloth, she didn't feel like having a shower anymore. It was cold in the bathroom, but an English nobleman showered even when it was cold. He ignores the cold, she thought. He doesn't allow it. She combed her hair, tied it up, and then shook it out again. She plucked a few eyebrows, sniffed her armpits, and washed her feet in the bidet. She squirted a bit of her new perfume on her throat. It smelled of a different country, of night and of love. Why not, she thought, he didn't insist on having a second bed, after all. An English nobleman, she had once read, used the sugar tongs, even if he is all alone. She had never seen sugar tongs. She pulled on her panties. Then she took them off again, and stepped into the room quite naked.

Christian was lying in bed. The television was on. An old film starring Catherine Deneuve. Kathrine slipped in beside him under the blankets, and pulled them up to her throat. Christian didn't look at her, only moved a little to the side to make room for her, and turned the volume down. She felt his nearness, and the warmth of his body. He asked if she wanted him to turn off the television. She said it didn't bother her.

"Isn't she beautiful?" he asked.

"What film is it?"

"*Belle de Jour*. Catherine Deneuve."

"If I was French, my name would be Catherine too. What does the title mean?"

"Beauty of the day," said Christian. "It's the story of a bored woman."

He looked at Kathrine. She smiled. She had never been bored, even though her life was monotonous, even though nothing happened in the village. Her favorite days had been the ones where everything was exactly as always. Only Sundays had sometimes bothered her.

Shots rang out on the television, and Christian turned to see what was happening. She turned away and shut her eyes.

When Kathrine awoke, it was light in the room. Christian was dressed, and sitting in a chair by the window. He was looking at his photos. Kathrine sat up in bed.

"Did you sleep well?" asked Christian.

"What about you?"

"I'm not sure. My girlfriend never stays the night. My parents . . ."

"But . . . ?"

"That was nice," said Christian, and held out a photo to Kathrine. She knelt on the bed to look at it. The cover slipped away, and she realized she was naked, and she felt ashamed. But Christian kept looking at the photo he was holding out to her.

"The aquarium at Vancouver," he said. "They had dolphins . . ."

He had sat down on the side of the bed next to her, and was flipping through the pictures.

"Killer whale. Squid. They're terribly intelligent. Have you ever eaten squid?"

"I wouldn't do that. I was in the aquarium at Boulogne."

She took the quilt off the bed, and wrapped herself in it. "It's cold."

"If you like, we can take the night train from Cologne to Copenhagen. Then we could spend another day here."

"Is that what you want to do with your life? Travel?"

"No," said Christian, "no." He thought about it awhile, and then he said no again.

It was a fine day in Paris. The city was very light, pale gray and silver. Belle de jour, said Kathrine.

"The Sacré-Coeur," said Christian, and pointed to the horizon, where a white church was shown in relief against the cloudy sky, "the blessed heart."

At five they were on the train.

In Cologne, they changed to the night train. They were on the platform far too early. They stood and waited silently, side by side. This is it, I'm going back now, thought Kathrine. We'll part at Kolding, and then I'll go home, what else is there for me? I'll go back to my apartment. Thomas will call sometime, or my mother. Thomas will ask where I've been, and my mother will say what did I think I was playing at, and poor Thomas, and didn't I think of the child at all? And then she'll tell me about old times, and the next time she sees Thomas she'll apologize on my behalf, and pretend it wasn't anything, and say I'd always been mulish like that. And he'll take my side, and that'll be the worst of it. Then she remembered she had sent in the lease, and that maybe there was someone else living there. She still had the key, but she didn't have an apartment anymore.

"Are you thinking about home?" asked Christian.

"Are you? Are you glad to be going back?"

"Yes and no."

Christian said he admired her. The way she managed her life, fought her way through, did what she wanted.

"What else am I supposed to do? I've got a kid. I have to earn money. What does that mean anyway, doing what I want?"

Christian said he was afraid of those things, renting an apartment, buying furniture, settling into a place.

"Why don't you move in with your girlfriend?"

"I can't make up my mind. I don't really love her. She's OK. She gets on well with my parents. And I suppose she's quite nice-looking." He laughed. "When I called my mother yesterday, she told me about meeting you. 'An odd woman,' she said, and 'Who was that?'"

"Do you think I'm odd?"

"No. You're something unusual. *Belle de nuit.*"

"Do you think I'm pretty? Did you tell her we were traveling together?"

"I don't think so!"

"Do you feel guilty about me?"

"We haven't done anything wrong," said Christian, looking serious, as though he had to convince himself.

Kathrine had to laugh. Then the train came. She saw people pushing their way through the narrow passages of the *couchette* coaches, and she was pleased that Christian had booked the more spacious *wagon-lits*. When the train moved off, she looked out of the window to get a last sight of the cathedral. She went into the compartment where Christian had already stowed the luggage away. The ticket inspector came and collected their tickets and passports.

"Up or down?" asked Christian.

Kathrine sat down on the lower bunk. He sat down next to her.

"I don't want to go back," she said, and after a while, "I want to sleep with you. Make love. What's that in French?"

"*Baiser*," he said, and got up. He went to the window, and opened it. Cold air filled the compartment. Christian stuck his head outside. Kathrine went up behind him. The wind scattered his hair. She put her arm round him. He screamed against the noise of the locomotive, a long, high scream like the noise of a locomotive. Like a child, she thought, he's like a child. She pulled him to herself, his body touched hers without wanting to. She tried to press herself against him. He resisted. She rubbed her face against his neck and for the first time sniffed his skin and his hair. Then she suddenly felt him yield, his body thrust against hers. He turned round and kissed her. He kept his eyes shut tight.

They made love without a word, just the occasional yes or no, like a movement of the hand, nothing else. Christian was different from the way Kathrine had imagined him, fast and powerful, and still with something shy or irresolute about him.

You can never quite imagine it, she thought later, it's always more or less than you'd thought. She wasn't sure if it had been more or less.

They lay together in the dark in the narrow *couchette*. Sometimes a light flashed by outside, and for a moment she caught a glimpse of Christian's face. His eyes were shut, and it was as though there was a man lying next to her whom she had never seen before. What she had seen of him before had disappeared, and what was left wasn't much more than a naked body, well built, almost too well, which gave it something lifeless. When she stroked his chest with her hand, the skin felt like packaging material.

"What are we going to do?" asked Kathrine. "What happens next?"

"Sleep," said Christian, "I'm tired."

And tomorrow we'll see, and she wondered if she had made a mistake, and then she thought what's done is done.

What are we going to do? That had been her mother's question in the year that had ended with them having to sell the boat. And her father said, I'm tired, and he had gone off to sleep. That was always the way she saw her father when she thought of him now, lying on the sofa asleep or dozing. The TV stayed on all day. Earlier, when they'd lived in Jukkasjarvi, he had always gone fishing in the streams. The fish are just there, he had said to Kathrine once, not like the reindeer, who all belong to someone, even though they run around freely. The fish really are free, they don't belong to anyone. That was after he'd been caught once, poaching a reindeer. He had cut off its ears, but the police had established that it had belonged to Per-Nils, his uncle. They had left Jukkasjarvi not long after. There wasn't yet enough money to pay for a boat, and her father had taken out a loan, which eventually ruined him. He didn't understand about sea fishing. He bought the wrong gear, and he overpaid for the boat. At first he was seasick whenever he went out, and he didn't catch much, and soon he couldn't keep up with the payments. They battled on for two or three years. Kathrine's mother worked in the fish factory, and the catches got gradually better. But then the fish stocks declined, and even the experienced fishermen didn't catch much anymore. If I can't catch a cod, I'll just have to catch a whale, her father said. Moby-Dick, he said, and laughed. He had never read the book. He bought a new sonar system, and some satellite navigation equipment, all on credit. But he didn't go out anymore. Then he began to drink. First, he went to the Elvekrog. When he no longer had the money for that, he bought black-market vodka from the Russian fishermen, and drank it at home. Sometimes he would get into his old Sami costume. Kathrine's mother asked him if he would call Per-Nils, his uncle, and ask him for help. I'll catch you a whale, said her father; that'll keep us fed for two years. A whale. And then he got sick.

The train drew into a station, and suddenly the compartment was brightly lit up. Kathrine woke up from her halfsleep. A couple of short-haired young men on the platform stared into the compartment, jeered, and waved their beer bottles. Christian had opened his eyes. He looked alarmed, but Kathrine pulled the blanket over him, and said don't mind them, they're just soldiers. When the train set off again, Christian stood up, drew the blind, and lay down on the top bunk. Dortmund, he said.

Half an hour before Kolding, Christian got up. His travel alarm clock went off, and Kathrine awoke and watched as he got dressed. When he was done, he approached the window. He didn't speak.

"We haven't done anything wrong," she said with a smile.

He turned and looked at her. There was a cruelty in his eyes that took her by surprise. He seemed to be furious with her, perhaps his conscience was hurting him, she didn't know. Like a child, she thought, but she didn't say anything, and he didn't say anything either. The train was already slowing down as Christian finally spoke. He spoke softly. His voice sounded as gentle as it always did.

"We shouldn't have done that," he said.

"Why not?"

"I don't know. It wasn't right."

"Were you thinking about your girlfriend?"

Christian didn't reply.

"I'm not asking anything from you."

"It's all so complicated," he said. "My girlfriend . . . I've got to talk to her, but . . . I always hoped things would be straightforward. That's all I ever wanted. But now . . ."

"Welcome to the world," said Kathrine.

He said he would write her an e-mail, and she repeated that she wasn't asking for anything from him. He kissed her on the cheeks, and she asked him, and maybe that was a mistake, but she just had to ask, did he like her at all, a little bit at least. Yes, he said, but now I have to go. I'll write you. Soon.

The train had stopped only briefly in Kolding, it had gone on, and two and a half hours later it was at its final destination—Copenhagen. There was just time for Kathrine to buy a ticket and a cup of coffee, and then she was already sitting in the train to Stockholm. From there, she would go on to Narvik, and take the Hurtig Line for the last stretch. She didn't have much money left.

When she reached Stockholm at four o'clock, it was dark already. She found an Internet café near the station. It was a bare room in a community center, with a few computers standing on long tables. Most of them were occupied by youngsters, who were playing a game. They proceeded, heavily armed, down a subterranean passage, and shot at everything that moved. It was dark. The changing light from the screens lit up the intent faces, which sometimes convulsed with shock or rage.

Kathrine checked her e-mail. She had been gone for almost two weeks, but there was very little in her mailbox. A pretty bland greeting from Morten on the day of her departure. Would she like to have coffee sometime. Some junk mail. Christian hadn't written yet. Kathrine thought about writing him, then she let it go. She called up the home page of the village, and its Web camera. At 30-second intervals, the pictures emerged, always the same view from the town hall across the square to the post office and the Nils H. Nilsen fish factory. In the background the Elvekrog, and on the foot of the slope on the left, various houses and huts. Once, someone came out of the Elvekrog, the open door made a pale area on the screen and a blurry shadow, only a few pixels big. Kathrine looked at it more closely, and started to see other, barely discernible shadows, the inhabitants of the village. Then she started seeing shadows all over, as if the whole village had turned out onto the square to wave to her, but that was a delusion, a flickering, maybe it was snowing. The camera wasn't very light-sensitive, and the image resolution was too low.

Kathrine read the latest village news. British journalists on visit to Nils H. Nilsen's plant, she read. Leatherstitching course in community center, soccer juniors triumph in Vadso.

She thought of Morten, sitting in his office, writing his little articles. He had made himself some coffee with his electrical immersion heater, had wondered whether he should go to the Elvekrog tonight, had looked up what was on TV. He had gone shopping on his lunch break, left his shopping at home, and managed to be back at work by two. On the town hall stairway there was a relief map of the Arctic territories, with the North Pole at the center.

Did Morten think about her at all? Another person disappeared, he wrote, a strange case. A young woman, a customs inspector by profession, well liked by all, with whom I spent a night, has disappeared, without leaving word.

What had she expected? Maybe Morten hadn't even noticed she was gone. The village might be small, but one could easily go several weeks without seeing someone. What about Thomas? Had he reported her as missing? And did he miss her? Did she miss him, her mother, Randy?

If someone was missing her, if someone was worried about her, it should be an easy matter to follow her traces. You won't find me, she had written on Thomas's note, but the Hurtig route would keep a manifest of its passengers, or you could ask the stewards, or the captains. Harald would be able to supply a description. And she had shown her passport around, and in Paris she had taken out the last of the money from her account. She had read thrillers, she knew people left traces unless they were very canny and experienced. And she hadn't been canny. She had known that no one would come looking for her. She was a free woman, who gave a damn where she was anyway. You won't bother looking for me, that's what she should have written on Thomas's note.

She logged onto a chatroom, but there were just a few crazies there, swapping perverted fantasies under assumed names. They must feel so pathetic, sitting in their living rooms, Kathrine thought. Their wives are asleep next door, and they're firing their dirty imaginings into the ether. I wouldn't like to meet them on the street at night, she thought, I suppose it's better if they lie and pretend to be decent people.

Kathrine thought about Randy, who had spent an afternoon as a deer. A game. She thought of the masks she had worn as a little girl, and of the masked balls at the Elvekrog. The sweat running down into your eyes, and your vision impaired by the narrow slits. Thomas had once come home with a pig mask, but he hadn't put it on. Kathrine imagined him in it. She looked into the narrow gap between the face and the mask, and she saw Thomas laughing uncertainly in the shadow of the other face, saw his pupils dart this way and that. She saw him standing alone in the lit-up room. She watched him from next door, the door was just ajar. He was standing there, naked but for the mask, with his upper body leaning back slightly. He grunted once or twice, first softly, then louder. Then he got down on all fours and crept around the room, and snuffled at the radiators, the furniture, the carpets. She saw him without a mask. Emerging from the bathroom, turning off the light, running to bed with short little steps, slipping under the covers next to her. She pushed the covers back. I want to see you. And all at once, Thomas had turned into a naked woman. He jumped out of bed, and ran off. He was an old woman, his skin was wrinkled, his hair white as snow. Stay here, she called after him. She got up. Thomas had vanished. All the doors in the apartment were open, the front door opened onto a snowy landscape. But it wasn't her apartment, and not her village.

Kathrine gave a start. A window had opened on the screen.

"You have a personal message from harrypotter," she read, "on your breasts are two fornicating frogs, two more frogs are fornicating on your thighs . . ."

She closed all the windows, paid, and left. The train to Narvik had left a quarter of an hour ago.

Kathrine ran through the streets of Stockholm. It was cold and rainy. People were clustered in front of the window of a television shop, watching a soccer game. Kathrine drank a coffee, and ate a hamburger. It was her first time in a McDonald's. She liked it. It was bright and clean, and all the surfaces were laminated, as they were in the room at the fishermen's refuge. Easy to clean.

In the corridor of the fishermen's home there was a map that showed all the missions up and down the Norwegian coast, clean, bright buildings, well heated, and easily washable. All the rooms were the same. The heating was electric, meals were served at the same time, the food wasn't good, but it wasn't bad either. And Svanhild took care of everything and smiled, if you asked a question. She wore a white coat like the workers in the fish factory, and she always had a rag in her hand. When she came to the table after the meal, to ask if it had been all right, she wiped her cloth over the table, and when you went to the register to pay, and exchanged a few words with her, she wiped her cloth over the counter, back and forth, without looking. Often Svanhild didn't say anything at all, and just wiped. Wiping was her language, it could mean anything at all.

In the village, people didn't know much about Svanhild. She came from the south of Sweden, that was agreed, and sometimes she told stories about that, stories in which she herself didn't play any part. It was as though she didn't have a life, had never had any life. She was very gentle, and she had a beautiful voice. If you asked her long enough, she would sing the sad songs of her homeland, and a big hush fell over the restaurant.

Only once had Kathrine seen Svanhild be vehement, and that was when a couple of seamen had brought beer into the fishermen's refuge. Svanhild had preached to them about the evils of alcohol, and when they laughed at her, she had turned them out.

She had never married. From time to time, directly or obliquely, a seaman would make a proposal to her, in jest or otherwise, and she would make a joke, and everyone laughed. When the seaman blushed and stammered, she would lay her hand on his arm and say, you need a young woman who'll have babies to occupy her while you're away at sea.

Kathrine followed a group of rowdy and laughing young people to a bar. The music was loud, and it was dark. Kathrine sat down at the bar, next to a woman who had her back to her. If someone looked at her, she smiled. But no one came and spoke to her. All the men she liked were with women, or in groups of other men. She smoked a cigarette, drank a beer. All around her there was laughter. The people knew each other, they often came here. And of course they didn't look at Kathrine, or just fleetingly, the way they might look into a shop window when the shop is closed, and move on. It wouldn't make the slightest difference if I wasn't here, thought Kathrine, and she smiled. She could smile in such a way that it looked as if she didn't care. I have to go back, she thought, I have no other choice. Take a job in Stockholm. Start a new life in Stockholm, or what people call a new life. But she was even more afraid of a new life than she was of her old one. Look for a job, an apartment. And where would she live until then? There was no fishermen's refuge here. Maybe the Salvation Army, a home for young women. But she wasn't a young woman anymore either. She was twice married, she had a husband and a child. She had to return.

Someone passed her a joint. She had never tried hash. Not with my job, she sometimes said. But she wasn't working now, and she felt sad, and perhaps a little curious. She took a drag, and was going to pass it on. But no one was sitting next to her, and so she took another drag, and then gave the joint back to the woman who had given it to her. The woman smiled and said, hey.

The music in the bar was lovely. There was something glassy about it, and the rhythm seemed to fit with Kathrine's heartbeat, her breathing, which kept accelerating. She made herself breathe more slowly, and before long she had the feeling she was only breathing out, or in and out simultaneously. It was as though she'd left the room, and was passing through a landscape, hovering over a landscape of sounds. When she shut her eyes, she saw brightly colored patterns that opened out like delicate fans or flowers. The patterns were yellow and purple and hemmed with black lines. They looked like gentle hills. It was beautiful, and Kathrine felt at ease. She opened her eyes and looked through a long tunnel or pipe. Someone had rolled up the carpet, with everything that was on it. Workmen had rolled it up, and carried it down to the street. Far away from her she saw people moving, getting up. But the music wasn't finished yet. Why did they turn out the lights, she wondered, and she closed her eyes again. She was rolled up inside the carpet, and slowly the cold got to her. The colors were gone. It was dark, and Kathrine was shivering.

"Where d'you live?" a man asked her. The door was open.

"Nowhere," she said, "I'm traveling." She looked at her watch. "I've got a train to catch."

She went to the station. Her mind cleared in the cold air. She was cold, but she was happy to be cold.

The train was already there, and she bought a ticket for a *couchette* from the conductor, and went into her compartment. She hoped she would be alone. One more night on a train, one more night in a *couchette*. Kathrine went out into the corridor, and looked out the window.

She felt sad and tired. She wanted to get back to her house and her village. She wanted peace. She wanted not to think for a while. She had seen so much in the last two weeks, so much that she had never seen before, and yet she had the feeling she hadn't seen anything at all. That people had different faces, she had already known. She had known that there are some houses that are bigger and more beautiful than others. A thousand times a thousand makes a million, and it wasn't necessary to go to Paris to find that out.

Hordes of downhill and cross-country skiers were walking along beside the train. They laughed and chattered. When the first of them climbed into Kathrine's carriage, she fled into her compartment, shut the door, and drew the curtains. She heard the skiers clatter past outside. Then the door opened, and three women came in. Each had a tin of beer in her hand. They were laughing. Their ski suits smelled of mothballs.

The three women were traveling up to Narvik together, to go on a skiing holiday. They all lived in Stockholm, they explained, and they drank their beer, and they talked about their husbands or their boyfriends, who all seemed to be idiots. When they learned that Kathrine came from the Finnmark, they asked her about Narvik, and about Norwegian men. They wanted to know if there were good pubs and discos in Narvik. There's a cinema, said Kathrine, and a library, and the three women looked at her with pitying expressions, and then spoke to her as if she were a child or handicapped person. They asked Kathrine where she lived, what her job was, if she had a boyfriend or even a husband. Kathrine said she had a child and a career, that she'd twice been married, that she was married to her second husband. At that the women were nicer to her. They introduced themselves: Inger, Johanna, and Linn. None of them had a baby, and they all worked in the same law office.

The four women got undressed. At first, Kathrine felt ashamed in front of the others, but then Johanna said something about Inger's paunch, and the three of them started to compare bellies and thighs, and they were amazed that Kathrine was so slim, and that there was no trace of her pregnancy. It was so long ago, said Kathrine. And she got a lot of exercise in the course of her work.

"You could make more of yourself," said Linn, who was lying on the bunk opposite Kathrine.

"My husband doesn't care," Kathrine said quietly. "It doesn't make any difference."

"That's what you say. And anyway, you'd just be doing it for yourself."

"I don't want to make anything of myself," said Kathrine.

Johanna, who was lying above them, told them to quiet down, she wanted to sleep, so that she'd be in shape for the Norwegian men.

"As if your Eirik ever gave you any peace," said Inger and laughed, "the bull of Lulea."

"Peace from his snoring, you mean," said Johanna, and gave a demonstration of Eirik's snoring. "No, honestly," she said, "I'm dead tired."

"Girls," said Inger.

Linn had gotten up.

"Scoot over," she said quietly, "or do you want to sleep?"

Kathrine slid over to the wall, and Linn crept in under the blanket next to her. Kathrine had never lain in bed with a woman. She had never had that many girlfriends, and the village was so small that there was never any reason to stay the night with one of them. You visited each other, stayed until late, but at the end of the evening you still went home.

Kathrine lay on her side, and Linn lay facing her. They both held their heads propped on their hands. Their faces were very close, and Kathrine lowered her gaze, and played with her hand on the pillow.

"Did you run away?" Linn whispered, so quietly that only Kathrine could hear.

"My husband lied to me," said Kathrine. "Everything he said to me was a lie."

"They all do that," said Linn. "You never know what you're up against. The best thing would be not to tell each other anything at all."

"I followed him once. He said he was going for a run. And then he was just sitting at the table in a hut."

"And you left him for that?"

"It was all lies. There wasn't a word of truth anywhere."

"Did he have someone else?"

Kathrine said that's what she had thought to begin with. But no, she was almost certain that he was faithful to her. If it had been that, she added, it would have been easier to understand.

"What about you?"

Kathrine said her arm was hurting. She turned to face the wall, and dropped her head onto the pillow. Linn pushed her head next to Kathrine's, and laid her hand on her shoulder.

"Your hair smells good," she whispered. "Do you use conditioner?"

"Tar soap," said Kathrine, and giggled briefly. "Once I had someone else . . . twice. We hardly ever slept together,

Thomas and I. Not for months. And then I met this old friend . . ."

"You don't have to apologize," said Linn.

"It felt so humiliating," said Kathrine, "the fact that he'd stopped wanting. . ."

"Are you crying?"

"I'm all right."

Linn said her boyfriend wanted to sleep with her the whole time. At first, she had liked it, but by now it was getting boring.

"He always does the same things. I think he has maybe three variations. After ten seconds, I know which it'll be. And if I don't feel like it, or if I have a headache, I mean really a headache, then he gets all offended, and says I have a problem, and I need to see a specialist. At least it's over quickly."

"Do you love him?"

"Men love. Women are loved."

Linn laughed softly, and asked what he was like in other respects, Kathrine's husband. Kathrine said she had no idea, everything he had told her was a lie.

"But you must know what he's like. I mean what he does, what he says, if he helps in the house, how he treats you when his friends are visiting. All that. He was around all the time."

Kathrine thought back. Then she said Thomas wasn't a bad man. He had aims, he knew what he wanted, and he was nice to the kid, even though he wasn't the father.

"He brings him presents, and me too."

"Well, what else do you want? And if on top of that, you've got this old boyfriend, with whom you . . ."

"I want a man I love," said Kathrine. "I want to love my husband."

"And now you're going back to him?"

"I don't know. Why did he lie to me so much?" Kathrine sobbed quietly. Linn drew her close, and stroked her head, the way Kathrine did with her kid when he was upset and couldn't sleep at night, and crept into bed with her and Thomas.

"I'd like to have a baby," said Linn. "What's it like to have a baby?"

"I don't know. He's going to school already."

"Why don't you stay with us at Narvik?" Linn gave Kathrine a gentle shaking, as if to show her something. "It would be fun. We've got two double rooms."

"I don't have much money left."

For a moment there was silence. Then Linn said Kathrine could come as her guest. The hotel wasn't very expensive, and she had a good salary, and it would be for her own benefit, it would be like a present to herself, because she quite often felt superfluous. Johanna and Inger had known each other long before she ever came on the scene, they had been friends at university, and they were a little older than her, and also they did downhill skiing, while she did cross-country. Kathrine was bound to be better at cross-country, so perhaps she could give her some tips, and interpret for them, and show them the sights of Narvik, only please not the library.

Linn talked for so long that Kathrine had changed her mind again, and was going to say no, but then Linn said, I like you, and Kathrine said, I like you too, yes, and thank you very much.

"You mustn't thank me," said Linn, gave Kathrine's shoulder another shake, and slipped off the bunk and back to her own bed.

At noon the next day, they had to change trains, and then the new train crossed the Norwegian border. It traveled through snowy valleys. Inger looked out the window the whole time, in the hope of seeing reindeer, and Johanna asked Kathrine questions about Norway that she was unable to answer.

The hotel was high above the station and close to the ski lift. The woman at the desk was red-cheeked and plump, and wore a traditional green dress, which Inger and Johanna laughed at as they all walked up to their rooms. Linn and Kathrine shared a room. From the window, they could see down to the fjord, and the black dockworks, where iron from Kiruna was loaded.

The next day, Kathrine borrowed a set of cross-country skis from the hotel, and went out onto the trails with Linn. When it had gotten dark early in the afternoon, the mountain with its illuminated slopes looked like a Christmas tree. The lights sparkled in the water of the fjord.

"It's beautiful," said Linn, "the night."

"Maybe," said Kathrine. "Come on, let's go back."

They ran into Johanna and Inger in the sauna.

"No men anywhere," said Johanna, but Kathrine was happy they were on their own. After the sauna, they rested, then they went out to a steakhouse. There at last they saw men, a group of Frenchmen, standing by the bar, who turned to look at the women when they walked in, and afterward too. When Inger went to the washroom, one of the Frenchmen began a conversation with her, and they could be heard laughing together. But then she returned to the table, and said, "What an idiot."

The three Swedish girls had never tasted reindeer meat. Kathrine said they should definitely try it. If only so that Inger finally got to see something of one. Inger and Johanna ordered hamburgers, but they tried some of Linn's and Kathrine's, and they had to admit the meat tasted good with the cranberry sauce on it.

After that, they went to the cinema, there was a science fiction film that none of them especially liked. But then what else were they going to do?

"The library's probably shut already," said Johanna, and grinned.

The four women walked through the night streets of Narvik. The snow had already melted away on the pavements, and refrozen, and melted again and refrozen, until it was an inch-thick sheet of ice. It had been sprinkled with gravel, but the four women kept slipping anyway, and held onto each other like drunks. They probably were all a bit drunk. They climbed up the steep little lane that led to their hotel.

"No men," said Johanna. "Norway is just as shitty as Sweden."

Johanna and Inger went inside, while Linn and Kathrine stayed outside, to smoke one last cigarette.

"She doesn't mean it that way," said Linn.

"How does she mean it?"

"Her boyfriend is a bastard. He throws himself onto anything that moves. He's come on to me before now. And Inger . . . he and Inger . . . ."

"Does Johanna know . . . ?"

"Yes, you should be pleased with the one you've got."

"I think I could have forgiven him for everything. But somehow it's past all that now."

"In our calling, if there's any doubt, it's innocent until proved guilty."

"But I'm not in any doubt," said Kathrine, and tossed her cigarette end across the street. "I always thought I didn't have any choice. And then when I was with Morten . . ."

"But basically, it doesn't matter what a man says," said Linn. "The main thing is having a good time."

"I realized that I don't really like Thomas," said Kathrine. "I never liked him, from the start," she said. "It's strange. I think I loved him. Or something like that. I wanted to stay with him. But I never liked him."

Thomas could never be a friend to Kathrine, just as Helge had never been her friend. She had never truly liked either of them, maybe that was why they had become her lovers, and then, a little fortuitously, husbands. Helge had been a wild man, and annoying because he never did what you asked him to. But Kathrine had soon realized that at the critical moment, he failed, drew in his horns. She had said as much to him herself. When it's a question of your personal advantage, you draw in your horns. And Thomas? Thomas had represented the chance of beginning a new life. No longer to have to work, to have enough money, to be able to travel. Kathrine thought of the big house, the many lovely rooms, the garden. She thought of the afternoons when she had been visiting, sitting in the garden and reading. And Thomas's mother had come out to her, offering homemade lemonade and cakes. She had sat down next to her, and embroidered one of her Bible verses, one of which she already had hanging in every room of the house. *I will dwell in the house of the Lord for ever.* Thomas's father, who had a Biblical citation for every situation, chose the verses, and Thomas's mother embroidered them.

"This is the one he chose for you," she said, and smiled. "We can hang it by the door to your apartment. Do you like the colors?"

Kathrine stayed for three days in the hotel with Johanna, Inger, and Linn. She took lots of photos. In the daytime, the four of them went skiing, in the evenings they went out to eat, and once they went dancing. There were even some men around, and they spent a cheerful evening together, but not more than that. Once, Kathrine wanted to go to the library, to look at her e-mail.

Morten had written to her. He hoped Kathrine would be back soon, he was missing her. She might at least say hello, wherever she was.

He doesn't sound too worried, she thought, but she didn't mind, and she wrote back quickly to say she was in Narvik, that she was fine, and would soon be back.

The others had had a look around the library by now. Johanna said there were probably more books than people who knew how to read. Just because we live up here doesn't mean we're thick, said Kathrine. Inger said she had once read somewhere that the brain activity of people in the North was diminished by the long evenings. "Just like with marmots," said Johanna. "They spend their summers getting fat, and in winter they sit around at home, watch TV, and commit incest."

"Did someone turn you down, then?" asked Linn.

"There isn't anyone there," said Johanna. "I wouldn't be in a position to get turned down by one of those fishheads anyway."

"Am I a fishhead, then?" asked Kathrine.

"There's nothing I can see, but it might still come," said Johanna.

That evening, the four of them went to a disco, and Johanna was aggressive again. Kathrine had danced with a man, quite close and quite long. And when she returned to the table where the other three were sitting, Inger said she thought the Norwegians were racists, because they didn't ask Swedish girls to dance.

"To look at you lolling there, no one would have thought you wanted to dance anyway," said Kathrine.

"Kathrine has more fun than we do," said Johanna. "Nothing in her purse to buy a beer, but full of good cheer."

Kathrine got up and left. Linn followed her to the hotel a few minutes later. Kathrine was sitting on the bed, crying. Linn sat down next to her, and put her arm around her.

"Johanna didn't mean it like that," said Linn later, as they were lying in their beds. They had the light out, and were talking a bit, as they had on the previous nights.

"I don't fit with you," said Kathrine.

"You fit with me, but maybe not with the others."

"I'm not more stupid than any of you. And as for not having any money . . . I'm going home."

"To your husband?"

"To my friends and my mother and my kid. Back to my village."

"Johanna has such a hard time with her boyfriend," said Linn. "He's a successful lawyer, and he puts her under a lot of pressure. He wants her to have a career like him. But she's not as good as he is. And then, as a woman . . . Inger is the best attorney of the three of us. I don't know what it's about. I don't care. But Johanna gets upset."

Kathrine repeated that she would leave in the morning, and she was a bit disappointed that Linn didn't try to talk her out of it. That might be the best thing, she said, it's a pity, but Kathrine should know what was best for her.

"Yes," said Kathrine, and then, "No."

"You can stay another day, can't you?" asked Linn. She had gotten up, and sat down on the edge of Kathrine's bed. "I'll pay, it's all right."

"The *Polarlys* is coming by tomorrow," said Kathrine. "I know the captain. I'd like to sail with him."

"Do you need money? Just say. You don't have to pay me back."

"No. I've enough."

"Can we stay friends?"

"Sure, if you like."

"I do like," said Linn, and kissed Kathrine. "I like you."

Kathrine had to leave early. Linn awoke when the alarm went off. She didn't get up, but she stayed awake, and watched Kathrine pack. Then they hugged, and Kathrine left. She took the early bus to Harstad, where the Hurtig Line boat was due to sail at a quarter past. On the *Polarlys*, she asked after Harald. He was still asleep. As she was sitting over breakfast, he wandered down into the dining room. He had shaved off his beard. He approached Kathrine's table with rapid strides, she stood up, and the two of them embraced like old friends.

They drank coffee together, and Kathrine told her story. Harald said he had told his wife about her stay. At first, she had been furious, but in the end she believed him, and now everything was all right again, perhaps even a bit better than before.

"We talked. At least that."

Then Harald had to go on duty, and go up to the bridge. Kathrine put away her luggage, and went up and joined him.

"Have you got a son or a daughter?" asked Harald. "And how old is your kid? And what's he or she called?"

"He's a boy. He'll be eight in . . . two weeks."

"And what's his name?"

"Randy."

"Tell me about him."

Kathrine said she didn't feel like it. She said she and Randy weren't particularly close. And never had been, she thought. She was so tired after the birth, by cesarean section, and then the postnatal depression, and her mother was there the whole time, looking after her, and giving her advice. Kathrine had found breast-feeding painful, she had gotten a breast infection, and Helge hadn't been any use at all, and had only offended her mother, until she stopped coming. Then things had gotten really difficult. Randy. Kathrine didn't like the name, even. It was Helge's idea, after some musician he liked. It hadn't been an especially good time.

"Tell me about him," repeated Harald.

"He's going to end up like his father," said Kathrine. "I once caught him torturing a dog."

"All kids do that."

"No, they don't," said Kathrine, "all kids don't do that."

"He's not to blame for his father. You chose him."

"And what if I did? He's still like Helge."

"Maybe he'll grow up, like Helge grew up."

"Did you study psychology?"

"My wife's like you. That's why I liked you straight-away. But . . ."

"But?"

"What's good for a man isn't necessarily good for a kid."

"You've got no idea what it means, bringing up a child. You're never home."

"You don't have to listen to me," said Harald, and turned away. "We don't have to talk, either. Look out the window. Maybe you'll see a seal."

They were silent for a long time. Finally Harald said, "Why did you marry him, if he's so awful?"

"We were OK together. As long as he was sober. And then the baby came along."

"They don't come by themselves."

"I slept with him. I didn't want to be alone, and I'd had a few. OK?"

"And even if he does turn out like his father, give him a chance, at least. It'll be hard enough for him, up there."

"Randy," said Kathrine. "My son Randy."

"And anyway, what did he do to the dog?" asked Harald.

The night they were supposed to reach Hammerfest, there was a storm. Over supper, the head steward went from table to table, and informed the few passengers that after ten thirty there would be rough seas for a couple of hours, but there was no danger. The captain apologized. But it's not the captain's fault, said Kathrine. But we always get complaints when there's a storm, said the steward, I don't get it either.

And in fact the storm began within fifteen minutes of the predicted time. Kathrine was surprised, but the steward said, it isn't the time, it's the place. We've steamed into the storm, and we'll steam out of it again.

The tourists had disappeared into their cabins, one by one. The lower deck was blocked off, but the doors to the upper deck were open, and Kathrine went out into the fresh air. She sat down on a chair that had been left out, and was slithering across the deck in the up and down of the waves.

All that could be seen was what the ship's lights illuminated. A small circle of light, the deck and the bridge and the rain showers, the spray in the air, which was not cold. The sea rose and fell, its movements were powerful but almost silent. What was loud were the wind and the diesel engines that were shaking the whole ship.

Somewhere out there were Alexander's men and the other fishermen. What about Alexander? He was dead, drowned, he wouldn't be back. What if I fell into the water, thought Kathrine, maybe one of the trawlers would fish me up. They would fish me up with a lot of fish, perhaps they wouldn't even be aware of it until they were back in port. But the sea was so big. And if you fell into it, the probability was that you would go to the bottom. No one was fished out. Lots of people drowned, but no one was ever found.

Kathrine stepped up to the rail. As the ship plunged into the waves, she saw the foaming sea below her. It would have been easy then.

Under the waves, the sea is quite calm, Christian had told her once. He had gone scuba diving in Spain or Portugal. You can swim under the waves, he had said, it's only immediately below the waves that you start to feel their movement. But underneath, it's calm and peaceful. All sound seems at once close and remote under water. Quiet, said Christian, but clear as glass. Kathrine knew that too, from the indoor pool in Tromso. That was where she had belatedly learned to swim, in the customs school, and she wasn't very good at it.

She thought of the fish moving in the depths, through the calm water, in darkness, suddenly being plucked up to the surface in a net, into the storm. Thousands of fish, squirming fish, pulled up onto the deck of the ship, an enormous body of fish, tipped into the hold, where they continued to wriggle and finally suffocated, or were killed by the fishermen. Kathrine thought of the tuna fish in Boulogne, with their old, earnest faces that looked almost human. She thought of how people died. Whether you continued to try and swim. The brief moment when you went down, before you suffocated. When you stopped struggling for breath, stopped thrashing about with your arms. The instant in which he'd given up, and maybe swam a couple more strokes, not to get to the surface, there was no point, and he knew it. A couple of strokes. And the calm, the quiet under the water. The fact that the last moment is supposed to be happy.

The ship was picked up by a wave, and Kathrine had to grip onto the handrail to avoid falling into the water. The sea was now a long way below her, she saw the gleaming hull of the ship, and the water streaming off it. Before the ship dipped again, she let go of the rail, and ran the couple of yards back to the door, and stepped into the little room.

Kathrine looked out the window. The storm was now almost silent, and it seemed to be a long way off. She wiped her hand over the cold glass, over the bumpy layer upon layer of gloss paint, the brass rails. All at once she felt very feeble, and sat on the floor with her head against the wall. For a long time she didn't think about anything, she wanted not to think about anything. She made slow circling movements with her hands over the fitted carpet. She thought, nothing can happen to me, I'm safe here. I'm going home now.

Finally, she stood up, and swayed through the long corridors of the ship, and down the stairs to the deck where her cabin was. The cheap cabins were all below the waterline. She heard the loud churning of the engines that drove the ship through the waves. For a moment, she thought of the gulf below her, the depth of the sea, death that was just a thin sheet of metal away. But it didn't frighten her anymore. She thought of how many times the *Polarlys* had made this trip, through how many storms that were much worse. It was a question of the place, not the time. She had never been afraid when she had flown to Tromso with Thomas and Randy. She lay on her bunk, and the ship rose and fell. Then, as suddenly as the storm had begun, it stopped. The next day the ship was once again sailing through calm waters.

"Are you worried?" asked Harald. "You're so quiet."

"It was my mistake," said Kathrine. "I cheated on Thomas. He was faithful to me. I lied to him."

"You didn't tell him everything," said Harald, "and you had every justification in sleeping with another man."

"Making love to another man, you mean," said Kathrine. She looked at the radar screen, on which the green shadow of the coastline was gradually moving past.

"You shouldn't be so dogmatic about lies," said Harald. "We all tell lies. What if you had never found out with him?"

"But I did find out."

"You would have been the happy wife of a rich and successful man, living in a beautiful house. Imagine."

"You mean I should go back to him, and pretend everything he told me was true?"

"Talk about it with him, and then forget it. It hasn't changed anything."

"If I could understand it. If there was a reason. But this . . ."

"What are we without our lies?" said Harald.

"It was so strange. You should have seen him, sitting alone at the table."

"You want to know everything, don't you? No secrets. What do you think you'd see if you cut someone open?"

Kathrine looked into Harald's eyes, and shook her head.

"Lies aren't secrets."

Kathrine sat on the observation deck. The room was almost dark. The ceiling was a man-made sky, with hundreds of little lights for stars. Kathrine thought of the evening she had lied to Thomas, and how easy that had been. She had lied to Helge before him. She had lied to her parents and her teachers. She lied every day, every hour. It wasn't hard. When her boss asked her about her weekend, when her mother asked her how her kid was doing at school. She even lied to herself. When she persuaded herself she was a good wife to Thomas, a good mother to her kid, that they were a happy family. That Randy didn't need that much attention, was happier on his own, or among his friends. That his eyes were OK, if there was a problem, he would grow out of it. When she had convinced herself that everything would turn out all right, even though she knew nothing was.

Actually, compared to her, Thomas with his little hiding place was a liar on an insignificant scale. How lonely he must have been all those months. As he sat at the table in his parents' hut, unable to go home, looking at his watch, how terribly lonely. And she hadn't understood him, and had left him sitting there. She hadn't been a good wife to him.

The *Polarlys* had sailed into the fjord, the lights of the village had appeared, and were getting brighter. The sea was quite flat. It was warmer than the air, and little mists formed over the surface of the water, rose up, and dispersed in the air. The ship was slowing down, and everything began to shake gently. The little glass tables on the observation deck jingled softly like glass bells.

Kathrine went up to the bridge, to say good-bye to Harald. He asked where she would spend the night. She said she didn't know where her things were.

"I can't let you leave the ship at half past one at night, not knowing where you're going to sleep."

"I'll find somewhere. They're all friends of mine, after all. I'm sure someone's still in the Elvekrog."

When Kathrine left the ship, she turned to look up at the bridge and wave, but she couldn't see anyone behind the dark windows. Good luck, Harald had said. She had forgotten to ask him why he had shaved off his beard.

Kathrine stood all alone on the dock. It was snowing gently. She didn't have money for a taxi, so she started to walk past the warehouses into the village. There were lights on in the windows of the houses. Kathrine passed the new hotel, the furniture store, and the shop for ship's electronics. She passed the police station, the old people's home, and the town hall. She stopped for a moment in the square in front of the post office. She looked back at the town hall and thought, if someone somewhere in the world has logged onto the village Webcam, they'll see me standing here. She was just a shadow, three or four dots high.

The door to the Elvekrog opened, and Kathrine heard laughter and singing. As she walked past the bar, she saw Helge standing on the street. He was reeling slightly, and fussing with his Harley. Kathrine stopped, and he turned and looked at her glassily. Hey, she said, how are you doing? Helge laughed. You didn't stick with him any longer than you did with me, he said, the woman's got no patience. You're a bad wife, but a good woman, he said. Oh, we had a good time. He turned and got on his motorbike, without starting it. Beauty of the night, said Kathrine softly, and then, louder, be careful, you shouldn't ride your bike when you're drunk. Helge laughed to himself, but he didn't say anything, and she went on her way. When she reached her mother's house, she heard the rattle of Helge's bike. She had a key, and her mother had a sound sleep.

The house smelled oddly familiar yet strange to her. Kathrine set her suitcase down in the hall, and went to the nursery, the room that had once been hers, and was now Randy's, when he was there. He was there, in bed, asleep. She watched him for a little while, and then she sat down on the little chair that had once been hers. The room looked small to her, everything looked small, the bed, the chair, the table, which had formerly been red, and which she had painted sky-blue. In some places, she could see the red again, and in some even the bare, gray wood. On the table were some yogurt cartons that were decorated with scraps of material and fur, and that probably had some significance for Randy, or for his schoolteacher. People, animals, houses, thought Kathrine, I'm sure they will have had something or other in mind.

The blinds were down, only the night-light shone in its socket, a little pinkish glow. Randy had always been afraid of the dark, even as a very little baby.

The pinkish light made his face look oddly stiff. What if he's dead, thought Kathrine. But his chest rose and fell slowly. Kathrine had never thought about it, but now she thought that she didn't want anything to happen to Randy.

Kathrine slept on the sofa in the living room. Her mother didn't wake her in the morning. When she got up, it was nine o'clock, Randy was at school, and her mother had done the shopping and made coffee. She said, you sleepyhead, you're sleeping through half the Lord's day. As she had always said, when Kathrine hadn't wanted to get up. She said a coffee in the morning will take away your worry and troubles. She said, there's supposed to be more snow on the way. And where have you been all this time?

"It feels much longer to me," said Kathrine. "It was only three weeks."

She had gone on a trip, she said, gone south. And that Thomas had lied to her. The letter had been his family's revenge. Is it not true then? No, it's not true.

"You always were an honest child."

"I spent a night with Morten."

That wasn't right of her, said her mother. Thomas had stopped . . . But her mother didn't want to know. He stopped sleeping with me. A marriage is a marriage. Then should Kathrine have stayed with Helge? You have to do what you think is right. I don't want to get involved in your life. Thank you.

But it wasn't an argument. Kathrine's mother didn't argue. She stood in the doorway, saying, Lordy, girl, the things you get up to, and then she went into the kitchen. Your things, she called out, are in the garage. Thomas brought them back.

"I'm going out."

"Will you be back for lunch?"

"Maybe."

It was snowing. Kathrine had always loved snow, and she loved it even more when fresh snow was falling. She walked through the village. The old women who were standing outside the fishermen's refuge with their Zimmer frames greeted her. The office workers came out of the town hall to drink Svanhild's coffee. Morten wasn't among them. Kathrine asked after him. He had taken the day off, presumably he'd skied out to the lighthouse. He'd been talking about doing that. He had bought some satellite navigation gear, and said he was going to try it out.

"What if it doesn't work?" said Kathrine.

His colleagues laughed and shrugged their shoulders. "He knows the way."

Kathrine went to the school. Even from a distance she could see the neon light outside the big classroom windows. The windows were stuck with brightly colored paper flowers that the children had made. Kathrine looked in at the window. She saw Randy sitting at one of the front desks. She was surprised. She had always imagined him as sitting at the back. He had a book in his hand, and was moving his lips. She could tell what a struggle it was for him to read. He was bending down over the book. His little body was all tensed up. Then the teacher went up to him, put her hand on his shoulder, and said something to him. Perhaps Randy did have something the matter with his eyes. The teacher had once made some reference to that, but Kathrine had never had the time to take him to the oculist at Kirkenes. Now she had the time.

She went up the steps and into the school. The smell of the stairway reminded her of her own school days, her fear of gym, of the other children, of her father, if she got bad marks. She remembered the mandarin oranges they stuck little candles in at Christmastime, and the teacher, who read stories aloud on Saturday mornings, about Stone Age children, and sometimes fairy tales. Kathrine went up to the door of Randy's classroom. She heard the voice of the teacher, and of one of the little girls:

Flowers red and white and blue
Blooming on the pasture green.
So that I may see them all,

I will walk right over them.
Right through the meadow.

But no, I had better not,
Because all those pretty flowers
Would be crushed and squashed . . .

Kathrine left the school again. They all come through
here, she thought. But when it's over it's over. Now he's
learning the same rhymes as we used to learn. What is my
baby doing? What is my little deer doing? Now I'll come
to you once more, and then never again. A fairy tale, which
one? Little brother and little sister. She had told it to Randy
once. About the spring that whispers, who drinks from me
will turn into a deer. Who drinks from me will turn into a
deer. And then the little brother drinks from it, and so he
turns into a deer. All afternoon, Randy was a deer, right
until supper, when Kathrine told him deer don't get to eat
ambrosia-creamed rice.

Kathrine walked to the cemetery. It was snowing harder
now. The houses all had lights on inside them, and some
of the windows still had Christmas decorations up, straw
stars, and strings of fairy lights, and lit-up plastic Santa
Claus masks. They hadn't had those when she was little.
There were lanterns lit in the cemetery. You couldn't see
the individual tombstones under the snow, but Kathrine
knew where her father lay. Her footsteps were the only
ones to be seen. From a distance, she heard the school bell,

and then the shouts and yells of the children as they ran home. Kathrine saw one or two from Randy's class walking up the hill. The children greeted her as she passed them on her way to the main street.

There weren't many trawlers at anchor in the harbor. Randy was standing with a couple of other children at the dock, watching a fisherman greasing a pulley. Kathrine called Randy, and he turned and ran to her. Silently, he took her hand. Together, they walked back to their mother, their grandmother.

"Do you like going to school?" asked Kathrine.

"I'm the second best at gym," said Randy.

"Were you learning a poem today?"

"All I can remember is the ending," said Randy, and he stopped, as though he couldn't walk and think at the same time. He stood in front of Kathrine, and breathlessly and earnestly recited the few lines he could remember:

I hope you stay there nice and bright!
Little flowers, I'll move on;
I just want to pick a bunch;
That's enough for me today,
Little flowers blue and white.

"Would you rather be blind or deaf or dumb?" asked Randy, as they took off their shoes outside the apartment door.

"What sort of question is that?"

"I'd rather be dumb."

After lunch, he ran out to play with the other children. Kathrine went into the garage. They had sold the car after her father died. Kathrine's mother couldn't drive, and Kathrine only had to for work. In a corner of the chilly building, next to the Deepfreeze, were a couple of large cardboard boxes, which Thomas had labeled "K" with his tidy writing, "K—books" and "K—kitchen," "K—kid" and "K—casual clothes." Next to them stood her cross-country skis. Kathrine picked them up, took them out, and slipped them on. Her mother came out to tell her to be careful, there was more snow on the way.

"Don't worry, I'll be careful," said Kathrine.

She set off in the direction of the lighthouse. Visibility was poor, but she knew the way. Once she had left the village behind her, and was over the first hill, she hit a track, almost covered over by the fresh snow. She followed it. Kathrine went for a long time. She wasn't cold, only her face felt chilly from the snow that was falling, harder now than before. She couldn't see the track anymore. It was getting dark again, and it wasn't even two o'clock.

An hour later, Kathrine saw someone coming toward her from a distance. It was Morten. She stopped. He had his head down pushing into the wind, and only saw her when he was a couple of yards from her. He got a shock.

"Does your new machine work?" she asked.

"Battery's gone dead," he said, with a grin. Then he said, "Hey, I'm glad you're back!"

They embraced, but didn't kiss. Their cheeks touched. Very cold, said Morten. But I don't feel cold, said Kathrine. You're not going out to the lighthouse, are you, asked Morten. Kathrine said she had gone out to meet him, and would come back with him.

"If you're hungry . . . ," he said. "And I've got some hot tea as well."

"You go on ahead."

Morten went on slowly, and kept looking around at her. At five they were back in the village.

"Do you want to come to my place?" asked Morten.

"Let's go to Svanhild's."

When Svanhild saw Kathrine, she came out from behind the bar, and, with a beaming smile, shook her hand. She asked where she had been, and wouldn't let go of her hand. She said Alexander's wife and his two daughters were there. She pointed to a table, where a plump blond woman sat, with a couple of girls almost as big as her. Kathrine recognized them from the photos Alexander had shown her.

"It's three months since he's disappeared now," said Svanhild. "On Sunday we're having a service for him in the church. We collected money so that they could come."

Maybe the woman would stay, she said. There was no shortage of work. The girls' names were Nina and Xenia.

Kathrine and Morten sat down at the table in the corner at the back, and Svanhild brought them coffee and homemade cake. The place was empty, apart from themselves and a couple of old workers from the fish factory.

"I've got some French cigarettes left," said Kathrine.

"And Paris is beautiful?"

"I'll show you my pictures, if you like."

"Why did you go to Paris, of all places?" Kathrine didn't answer. Then she told Morten about Christian, and that she had slept with him on the train. Then it was Morten's turn not to speak.

"You weren't there when I went away. I went looking for you, and you weren't there. Are you jealous?"

"What do you think?"

"I don't want to lie to you."

Kathrine told him about Stockholm and Boulogne, and how she'd eaten shellfish for the first time in her life, and smoked dope for the first time. Morten listened and he laughed, but she sensed he was different from how he had been before.

"I have to get used to the fact that you've slept with him," he said.

"I slept with Thomas as well."

"That was a long time ago. Anyway, he's your husband."

"And with you. And you're not my husband."

Morten nodded. He said that, to begin with, they had thought she had done herself a mischief by disappearing like Alexander. Thomas had run to the Elvekrog, all excited, and said they had to help him find his wife. He really said his wife, as if they didn't all know who Kathrine was. Then when they had gone down to the harbor and asked after her there, the harbormaster had said he had seen her leave on the *Polarlys*.

"And you just stopped looking for me after that?"

"You're your own woman. You can go wherever you like."

"I was afraid someone might try and keep me from going. I don't know. I had the feeling I was doing something wrong. I felt like a criminal on the run."

"I thought you wouldn't come back. Most of them don't come back."

Morten said he had lately been thinking quite a lot about leaving. He knew some people at the national radio, and he could probably get a job in Tromso, or even in Oslo. Couldn't she get herself transferred? If she got her job back, she might be able to, said Kathrine. Tromso, why not. That might have been the happiest time in her life, those months in the city, with her male and female colleagues, the parties, the cinemas.

"Why not," she said. "Would you want me to go?"

"We wanted to leave together when we were kids."

Then she asked him what had happened, when they had stowed away together to Mehamn. Ha, said Morten, and then he told her the story.

And then they stood around uncertainly outside the fishermen's refuge, and Morten asked again if she wanted to come up to his place, but he didn't seem to be too sure about it. Helge rattled past on his Harley, and Kathrine said, no, she'd better go home. She wanted to see Randy, whom she'd neglected for so long.

Randy was a funny boy, said Morten. "Two weeks ago, I had his whole class in the studio. I talked to them about how you make a radio program. We recorded a little show, and Randy was the announcer. He was really good."

Kathrine asked Morten if he could make up a tape for her, and he said he would.

"Sometimes," he said, "when I listen to my shows, I think maybe no one's listening at all. And my voice goes past all the houses, and out of the village, and as far as the transmitter reaches. It's a weird feeling."

Kathrine nodded. Then they parted.

Kathrine went to the customs office. Her boss was still there. He was sitting in his office, smoking, and reading the newspaper. He was happy to see her.

"I've got my sister-in-law and her husband visiting, and their three awful children," he said. "So I'm doing a lot of overtime."

"Why don't you go to the Elvekrog?"

"My wife doesn't believe me. She calls here to check up on me."

Kathrine asked if anyone had been taken on in her old job. No, said her boss. She hadn't given in her notice. He had asked for unpaid leave for her, first one month, and then a second. But if she wanted to start again before that time was up, that was fine by him. Head office had sent along this guy from Vadso, a real stickler, who didn't get along with the Russians. He was staying at Svanhild's, and would probably be relieved to be able to go home. "Tomorrow?"

"Thanks very much," said Kathrine. "What about next Monday? I've still got lots of things to sort out."

Then her boss asked if she was back together with Thomas, and immediately he apologized, it wasn't any of his business of course, but . . .

"But what?"

"We wondered about your taking off just like that."

"Hardly just like that."

"You mean the letter?"

"I think we've said enough."

Yes, said her boss, and got up. He said he was happy she was back with them, and she said she was too. They shook hands. He walked Kathrine to the door. When she was already outside, he asked, "Anyway, where did you go?"

"I'll show you the pictures."

On her way home, Kathrine thought about the journey from Paris to Boulogne. She had taken pictures out of the window of the train. Blurry landscapes, an overcast sky, now and then a few houses, a village. A narrow road that went along next to the track for a while, two women on horseback, a cemetery. But there were also things you couldn't see in pictures: stopping in places whose names she'd never heard of. A place called Rue, which meant road. Then the landscape got very flat. The train crossed a river with hardly any water in it. When she went back the other way, it was full of brownish water. The floods, Christian had said.

Her free days went quickly. On the street, Kathrine was asked whether she had gone on holiday, and sometimes she showed people the pictures from her time away, and she barely recognized the places anymore. Once she saw Thomas coming toward her on the pavement. When he saw her, he turned and disappeared around the nearest corner. That night, his father called. Kathrine's mother answered the phone. She was friendly in her submissive way, asked after the family, how they all were. Then Kathrine took the receiver out of her hand and asked him what was going on.

"I don't know what Thomas has been saying," she said. Then Thomas's father talked for a long time. She listened, two or three times she said something. It's his own fault. No. Yes. There are some things . . . I don't want anything. He should just leave me alone.

"I don't care if he wants a divorce or not," she said. "He's not my husband anymore. Doesn't matter what it says on the piece of paper."

Her mother stood next to her. Her alarmed expression made Kathrine furious. When she hung up, her mother started to cry.

"Stop that! You should be happy it's all over."

"But what will people say? Not yet thirty, and twice divorced."

"He doesn't want to get divorced. We don't do divorce, his father said. We." Kathrine laughed aloud.

"But think of Randy," said her mother.

"I am thinking of Randy. And I'm not having him going up there anymore."

"They want to have a birthday party for him."

During that week, Kathrine and Morten didn't meet, but Morten sent Kathrine an e-mail every couple of hours or so. He must have gotten hold of a French dictionary from somewhere, because he was writing things she didn't understand that still made her laugh. In the evenings, they talked endlessly on the telephone.

"Was your grandmother really French?" Kathrine asked once.

"She was a Sami. So was my grandfather. My father still lived in a tent. He used to tell me about it a lot. How cold it was. When they built the house, he was five. And when they moved in, Father said, now we're in Paradise. In the summer they went up in the mountains with the reindeer."

"My father was a Sami as well," said Kathrine. "Why didn't you ever mention it?"

"My father had a cassette with songs. And if someone couldn't sleep, he put it on. Voi, voi, voi . . ."

"Stop it," she said. "Why didn't you ever say?"

"What does it matter. Do you want me to go around in a red hat?"

The next day, Kathrine asked her boss about getting transferred, and Morten called all his friends in Tromso, to ask about work. On Saturday, he took the Hurtig Line boat. Kathrine came along to the harbor. Morten was the only passenger to join the boat.

"Finnmark Radio," he said, "well, we'll see. They're not really looking for anyone. On the other hand, they liked my show. We'll see."

"When are you coming back?"

"When I've found a job. Shall I call you when I'm in Tromso?"

The next day, it was the service for Alexander. Kathrine went to church for the first time since her father's death. The evening before, she had met the woman who had been the last person to see Alexander alive. Kathrine had asked her if she was coming, but the woman said, better not.

Her mother was coming along, even though she had never met Alexander.

"He was a fisherman," she said, and Kathrine said, "We don't know he's dead."

They took Randy with them. He sat between them, and was very quiet. The reverend talked about Jonah and the great fish.

"For thou cast me into the deep," he said, "in the midst of the seas; and the floods compassed me about; all thy billows and thy waves passed over me. The waters compassed me about, even to the soul; the depth closed me round about, the weeds were wrapped about my head. I went down to the bottoms of the mountains; the earth with her bars was about me for ever; yet thou hast brought up my life from corruption."

Kathrine looked at Alexander's wife and his two daughters, who were sitting in the front row between Ian and Svanhild. Presumably, they didn't understand a word. The girls shifted about. They had thin braids, tied with colored ribbons, and they wore clothes that looked as if their mother might have sewn them herself.

Then the organ played, and the preacher said, "Overnight we are created, and overnight we are unmade again."

Kathrine couldn't remember what the minister had spoken about at her father's funeral. She had felt paralyzed the whole time, and had only been able to cry when they were back at home. "In the night Alexander Sukhanik left our village, and he has not been seen since," said the minister. "We do not know where he is. But wherever he is, he is with God, and God is with him. Because no sheep is ever lost from His flock."

Kathrine didn't believe what the minister was saying, and yet his words were comforting to her. Perhaps it was enough if he believed it, or Alexander's wife believed it, or Ian or Svanhild. Perhaps it was enough if the minister just spoke the words. Perhaps it was enough that they were all assembled here, that they were thinking of Alexander, that they would remember him later, and this day and this hour.

After the service, the minister and Alexander's wife and Ian stood by the door, and everyone went past them, and shook the minister's hand and the wife's. Kathrine thought of saying something, but in the end she didn't, and she just shook hands with the woman.

"My husband was a fisherman as well," said Kathrine's mother. Ian whispered something into the ear of Alexander's wife, and she nodded and smiled.

After a week, Morten still wasn't back. On Sunday it was Randy's birthday. Kathrine hadn't finally had the heart to put a stop to the party at Thomas's parents. She took Randy there. She stopped at the garden gate. Behave nicely, she said, don't eat too much, and say thank you for your presents. She watched Randy running across the big garden, and she thought he's small for his age, but he'll grow. As she was on the point of going, Thomas's father stepped out of the house.

"Kathrine," he called out, "we have one or two things to settle."

Kathrine hesitated. Then she thought, I'm not going to run away a second time, and she went up to the house. Randy had slipped past Thomas's father, and had disappeared inside. From the passage, Kathrine could see into the living room, where Thomas and his family and a dozen or so of Randy's classmates were all sitting. Over the door was a banner, with "Happy Birthday" written on it in bright colors. The living room looked cozy. It was decorated with paper chains, and there were presents lying on the table, along with big dishes and bowls full of cakes and sweets. Randy was very excited. He had his hands clasped in front of his chest, and he was shaking them this way and that. He turned round to look at Kathrine. She nodded to him. The guests sang Happy Birthday.

"We'll go in the study, shall we?" said Thomas's father.

They sat opposite each other. Thomas's father lit himself a cigar, rather fussily. It's you who want something from me, thought Kathrine, not I from you. Nothing can happen to me. I'll just sit through this, whatever it is, and then I'll go, and I'll never come again.

Thomas's father told her not to be stupid. Thomas was a good man, and he meant well by her. He had spent weeks getting the apartment ready. He had ordered furniture all the way from Oslo. She must see how lovely everything was. Would she like to see it? And for Randy too. His room had been turned into a little boy's paradise. Thomas had bought a computer for the kid. It was important that kids learned early on how to work on computers, because that was the future.

"The future is in the children," said Thomas's father. And when she spoke about Thomas's lies, he said, "You must look to the future. Don't always look back. We've all made our mistakes."

The letter? A piece of nonsense. Thomas's father apologized for it. Thomas had insisted she had done it with other men. Excuse the expression, he said, how could we know . . . That he was lying? That he wasn't telling the truth. It must be in her to forgive a man.

"You who put your faith in Him will understand the Truth," said Thomas's father, "and the faithful in love will live with Him."

"I don't want to forgive him," said Kathrine, "and I don't love him."

Thomas's father said that could surely change. He and his wife had some difficult times behind them. Enduring love was the invention of romantic novelists. Marriage was an institution, it was what society was founded on, its smallest cell. And she should think of Randy.

"Thomas is ready to adopt him. Randy would be our only grandchild. The way things are looking with Veronica and Einar, he might well remain so. Think of what possibilities would be open to him. It's not just the house. I'm going to be quite open with you. My fortune is much greater than just this house. We have papers, secure investments. And on my wife's side, a lot of land. All that will belong to Thomas and Veronica, and then one day to Randy. Don't be silly. What more can you want from us?"

"No," said Kathrine, getting up. "I can't ask for any more."

As she stepped out of the study, she saw Randy kneeling on the floor in a pile of presents and brightly colored wrapping paper. He was just opening a present. He looked serious and intent. Kathrine went into the living room. The grown-up conversations all stopped, but the children went on talking and playing on the floor with those things that Randy had already unwrapped. Kathrine looked over at Thomas. He slowly got to his feet, beckoned to her to sit in one of the armchairs, and smiled solicitously. Kathrine went to Randy and said, Come on. Randy looked up at her. She held out her hand. I haven't finished unwrapping everything, he said. Come on, said Kathrine. Tears were running down her cheeks.

"Come on," she said softly, "we're going now."

Randy didn't want to go. No, he shouted, and then he started crying and screaming. Some of the other children started crying too, and Kathrine snatched Randy up, pulled his jacket off the hook in the hallway, and left the house. Only when they were out in the garden did she set Randy down, put on his jacket, and take his hand.

"Those are bad people," she said. "We're never coming here again, do you understand?"

Randy was still whimpering, but he walked home with Kathrine.

Morten came back from Tromso two days later. The thing with the job at Radio Finnmark hadn't worked. He had gone round to some other employers, and finally got a job at an Internet company. A good job, he said, they would like me to start right away, but I can't start before the beginning of April. What about you? Next June, said Kathrine. A colleague is taking maternity leave, and I'm keeping her job warm. After that, we'll see.

"I'll get a room," said Morten, "and when you come, we'll look for an apartment together."

Kathrine had gone round to Morten's for the first time since getting back from her journey. They had cooked a meal together, and eaten and washed up. Afterward they sat at the kitchen table, and worked out how much rent they could afford, and they looked at ads in the papers that Morten had brought back from Tromso with him.

"Two children's rooms," said Morten. "What do you think?"

Kathrine was sitting in the fishermen's refuge. She had finished her lunch. Her colleagues had gone back to work, but she was still sitting there, as though waiting for something. She looked out and saw the village, as though for the very first time. Morten walked by outside. She waved to him, but he wasn't looking, and didn't see her.

That evening, Kathrine was back in the fishermen's refuge. She was looking out the window. In the parking lot outside, there were some cars with their engines running, with pale young men sitting in them, sometimes alone, sometimes in pairs. She knew most of them but only by sight. They were too young, their parents too old. There were families in the village who never met.

In a red Volvo sat a man and a woman. The woman was talking and waving her hands about, the man was looking down, he was smoking a cigarette and listening to her. After a while he got out of the car, threw away the cigarette, and walked off. The woman in the Volvo punched the steering wheel with her fist, and then she drove off.

In the hall, one of the Russian seamen who was staying there was telephoning. He was speaking English. Kathrine could understand what he was saying. She smiled.

From the television room, she could hear an announcer reading out the lottery numbers. Five, eleven, thirteen, thirty-one . . . Kathrine wondered what Svanhild would do if she won the lottery. She herself had never played, she had no idea what she would do with the money. Perhaps go on a trip. Helge had used to play, Thomas too, even Morten occasionally.

April, May, June, Kathrine counted them off. Helge, Thomas, Christian, Morten. Three thousand kronor in her bank account, a few books, a few clothes, a few bits of kitchen equipment. A laptop. A kid.

Randy was eight now. Kathrine was twenty-eight. She had lived here for twenty-one years, almost a quarter of a century. She was afraid to leave the village. But Morten would help her. He had lived in Tromso once before. They would look for an apartment together, buy furniture, maybe a car sometime. They would go out to restaurants and films together.

Kathrine got coffee from the sideboard, left five kronor next to the till, and sat down at the window again. Goodbye, said the Russian seaman in the hall, three, four times, before hanging up. A door slammed shut, the television was switched off, and nothing was audible beyond the humming of the fridge and the quiet ticking of the wall clock. Svanhild stood by the door, turned off the light, and then on again. She apologized. I didn't see you. That's OK, said Kathrine. She finished her coffee, it was only lukewarm now, and she said good night, and went.

She walked through the village, and then along the road that led to the airport. She counted her steps up to a hundred, ten times, and then she gave up. Beyond the old airfield were the huts, the hut where Thomas had sat waiting for whatever he was waiting for. Kathrine wondered what would have happened if she had gone in to him. Maybe he had been waiting for her.

Now, at night, the distances seemed shorter than they did by day. The snow was light, it was as though the earth was glowing under the dark sky. Kathrine thought about Randy's pinkish night-light. The bright spot in the dark room.

The air was very clear and cold. Clouds came up and moved over. Then she could see the stars again. And then Kathrine saw the Northern Lights. Like a fine curtain right across the whole horizon. Kathrine waited, watched as the wide veil grew narrower and glowed more strongly. Suddenly it was just a thin strip, a quivering green line, a snake twisting wildly in the sky.

Lucky me, she thought. She felt cold, and she went back.

On the edge of the village, she passed a group of Russian seamen, who were probably on their way back to their ship. As she passed the fishermen's refuge, the lights were all off. Only one room on the lower ground floor still had its light on, that was the window to Ian's little chapel. Kathrine looked in. She saw Ian walking past the row of empty chairs, collecting up hymnals. She knocked on the window. Ian jumped, but when he saw her face in the window, he smiled, and waved to her.

Linn sent Kathrine an e-mail as soon as she got back to Stockholm, and Kathrine wrote back to say she was fine again. Thereafter, they didn't write each other that often, but every now and again. And once, when Kathrine and Morten were living in Tromso, they drove to Stockholm, and met Linn, who was now living with Johanna's Eirik, and was complaining about him. And years later, when Linn was on her own again, she came to Tromso, and stayed with Kathrine and Morten for a few days, and they talked about their skiing holiday, and how they had met, and everything that had happened.

Christian never got in touch. He didn't send any e-mails or any more postcards. Once, Kathrine wrote to him, and he wrote back, saying he'd got married, and he wished her well.

Then Kathrine visited her mother in the village. She took the *Polarlys* with Harald, who was going to change to a newer ship, and had separated from his wife, or she from him. He had grown a beard again, and there were even more burst veins on his cheeks now. Kathrine and Harald stood side by side as the *Polarlys* sailed into the fjord, and watched as the lights of the village appeared above the spit of land.

Kathrine counted them up. A trip to Stockholm, a voyage to Sicily, a honeymoon, summer holidays in Jotunheimen National Park, visits to the village.

Her mother had gotten old. She complained more and more about the darkness and the cold. Why don't you move down to Kiruna, to your family, suggested Kathrine. But her mother didn't want to leave the village.

"Someone has to stay here," she said.

Ian, the Scottish priest, had hanged himself one night in the waiting room for the Hurtig Line. The harbormaster had found him the next morning. His body was cremated, and the ashes were sent back to his family in Scotland. That was what he had wanted.

"I don't want you to burn me," said her mother. "You must bury me here, next to Nissen."

"Stop it," said Kathrine.

Her mother only talked about Thomas when Kathrine asked. After the divorce, he had married a worker in the fish factory, who had left him a year later. There was some talk in the village. Then he had left the village. His parents were still there, but they led a very withdrawn life. They didn't even say hello when her mother met them on the street.

Alexander had never been found. But his wife was now working in the fishermen's refuge, helping Svanhild. The two girls, Nina and Xenia, helped there as well. They had both grown a lot, and were speaking Norwegian, as if they'd been born here. They were pretty girls, and for a time, more young people came to the fishermen's refuge. Svanhild often sat at a table in the kitchen. All that standing around had made her tired. She sat at her table, and smiled, and wiped her cloth over the gleaming plastic surface without looking.

Alexander's wife had saved some money, then a year ago, she had put up a stone in the cemetery, and the minister had held a service for Alexander. Now everything was fine.

Kathrine went to work. She took the car. She dropped Randy off at school. He got sick, and then he was better again. He got a pair of glasses. He grew tall. Kathrine earned money, and bought things for herself. She had another child, a girl this time. Solveig. Then she stood in the kitchen with Morten. They made sandwiches to save money. Later, they bought an apartment, and one day a house. They lived in Tromso, in Molde, in Oslo. On his holidays, Randy went up to stay with his grandmother in the village. He came back. It was fall, then winter. It was summer. It got dark, and then it got light again.